GEORGE
GOOD FRIEND
AND A PART IN
THE MOVIE

R. b. Hay

Fire Horses

R.J. Haig

ISBN 0-7414-4267-1

Published by:

INFINITY
PUBLISHING.COM

1094 New DeHaven Street, Suite 100
West Conshohocken, PA 19428-2713
Info@buybooksontheweb.com
www.buybooksontheweb.com
Toll-free (877) BUY BOOK
Local Phone (610) 941-9999
Fax (610) 941-9959

Printed in the United States of America

Printed on Recycled Paper

Published November 2007

Acknowledgments

I want to thank my wife Jo and all those people who encouraged me to keep going when I was writing "Fire Horses". A special thank you goes to Local 344, The Detroit Fire Fighters Association, for their efforts in protecting us from those who tried to destroy our unity. The Detroit Firemen's Fund Association will always be a part of the heritage that keeps us connected. Thank you Fund officers, past and present. Most important is my favorite newspaper man Bill McGraw. Thanks Bill for encouraging me to be myself ....Bob Haig professional Firefighter writing about Firefighters.

This novel is a fictionalized compilation of the type of situations Firefighters find themselves involved in everyday. I thank the Lord for allowing me to be among these heroic special people for thirty years. I know they will identify with many of the actions contained in the pages of this book.

Chapter One

There was this old firefighter I once knew who hung around Casey's bar. His name was Jack Montgomery. He had long white hair and a mountain man beard. His eyes were sad and droopy but always twinkled when he talked about the old days. He was ninety years old and his mind was sharper than the peen of an axe. He could have passed for a hippy if he wasn't so old.

All the guys loved Jack He was one of the few retired firefighters whose career went back to the horse and buggy days. If you bought Jack a beer he would talk about times when the duty shifts were long and the bosses were tough. Jack told stories of big fires and life in the fire house when the building was shared with horses. It was a time of brass spittoons, tin fire helmets, and steam fed pumpers. His stories were long. He always worked his listeners for that extra beer. It was fun to listen to Jack. I enjoyed his stories about the fire horses most of all.

He said the horses were cared for better than the firefighters. They were big animals. The department used draft horses like the ones you see in the Budweiser commercials. The men loved these horses and gave them special care. They were groomed and well fed at all times.

Jack said they had a horse named Charlie who worked out of Engine 32 on the east side of the city. This horse had a sense of humor. He had inherited the practical joke mentality of his firemen friends. Charlie had a favorite trick. When a man would come into his stall to brush him down the big horse would gently lean sideways and pin him to the wall. He would hold him there until the man cursed and yelled before freeing him. This was terrifying for the rookies who did not know the old horse's tricks. Jack said Charlie would roll back his lips and smile after letting a man go. It was a goofy smile because Charlie had a big front tooth missing. In all his years on the job, Jack said Charlie was the only horse he ever knew that could smile.

Over time the horses learned to identify the alarm box numbers as they came in over the ticker tape alerting engine 32 for a run. When a call came in the horses were instantly energized. Their eyes would blaze in anticipation. They would move to the front of their stalls stomping and snorting ready to go. Jack said that Charlie would prance up and down in a stutter step and would have that goofy smile on his face. Once the chains in front of their stalls were removed the horses would move quickly to the front of the pumper for harnessing. Once they were harnessed and hooked up the horses would tremble and shake waiting for the command to go.

Out the door they would come crashing and clattering. Firemen would be hanging to the sides and rear rails putting on turnout gear. Most fire companies had a dog and he would run next to the horses barking and howling. It was an impressive sight to see a steaming pumper going to a fire. One thing for sure, you knew they were coming.

I was thinking about Jack Montgomery and the fire horses as we drove toward town this evening. My favorite tale was about how they retired the horses when they became too old to work. Jack said they took the horses to Belle Isle. Belle Isle is an island that sits in the Detroit River about a quarter mile off shore. The island is two miles long and can be seen from Engine 32's quarters on the mainland.

Jack said the retired horses were kept in a large pasture that bordered the river. During the day the horses could be seen standing silently under the trees staring across the river at the fire station. When Engine 32 would get a fire run the horses would rear and snort. When the steaming pumper came roaring out and started down the street the horses on the island would take off running. They would gallop full tilt parallel to Engine 32 until they came to the end of the pasture. They would buck and whinny like young colts. Jack said they never lost their desire to go to a fire.

Jack swore that many years later, when the city converted to motorized fire rigs, the ghosts of the horses were still on the island. He claimed on foggy nights, when Engine 32 was responding to a fire, the guys on the back of the rig would sometimes say they thought they saw horses running on Belle Isle.

At this point we would laugh and tell Jack he was drinking too much beer. It was strange how the thought of those horses was on my mind tonight. There is something mystic about memories, spirit, and desire. They are intangibles but do they have substance? I know in my heart I am still a firefighter even though I retired two years ago. Would I still like to go on a fire run? You bet I would.

Chapter Two

It is my belief that retired firefighters and retired fire horses have the same feelings. Memories are not only stored in the brain; they are kept in the heart. Shared experiences create a special bond for those who work in this profession.

There is a rite of passage when a person comes on the job. A rookie is called a trial firefighter and it will be six months before he gets his badge He must pass many tests before he is accepted into the brotherhood. His bosses and senior men will literally hold his hand as he goes to those first few terrifying fires. At the fire house he gets all the dirty jobs. He is low man on the totem pole and will have to prove himself before he is accepted as an equal. A trial man learns he has two families, one at work and one at home. A bonding is created that is carried to the grave by all who experience it.

These things flowed through my mind as I reflected on my thirty years with the Detroit Fire Department. I hung up my helmet and retired two years ago. I missed the action and camaraderie but my body could no longer take the pounding required to be an active firefighter. I was now living with my wife Jo on a farm in northern Michigan. It's a peaceful place. We have 160 acres of woods and fields. The only action I see is when our boys come up hunting in the fall. Some nights we can hear the coyotes howl. Their distant mournful cries remind me of the sirens heard at night in the city. That's as close to fire fighting as I get now of days.

Yes I still missed it and that made this evening special. We were on our way to a wedding in Cheboygan. The grand daughter of Mac Pierce was marrying a local kid. The reception was to be held at the Knights of Columbus Hall at the south end of town. Mac retired six years ago and was now running a party store at the edge of town. He is a jovial person who likes to talk to people. Owning a store was a perfect fit for his personality. He was the Captain of Squad 4 when he was on the department. He was a great boss and a fearless firefighter. Mac's main virtue was his steadiness under stress. He never got rattled.

I was in high spirits. It was going to be a special evening for the retired firefighters who had been invited. It would be a reunion of old running mates. It was going to be fun to see the guys again. It was two years ago since we were last together. I understood there would be six or seven of these over the hill smoke eaters at the wedding. I knew for sure Joe Barchilli and Danny O'Brien were going to be there.

Danny stood six feet tall. He had long curly black hair and flashing blue eyes. Danny was always smiling. He loved life. He was trim and fit. He could drink gallons of beer and eat tons of cheese burgers and never gain an ounce. He was playful as an otter. The room would fill with excitement when Danny walked in.

He didn't look for trouble but if it came he never backed down. Over the years I had seen Danny take on guys twice his size. He didn't always win but those he fought knew they never wanted to fight Danny again. His carefree attitude and let the party begin smile made him a favorite with the girls. He was a heart breaker because he never responded to any flirtatious encounters. Danny married his high school sweetheart and never strayed from his promise to be faithful. He was moral as a priest, goofy as a clown, and tough as a wolverine. He was my best friend.

Danny was a fun guy. We grew up in the same neighbor-hood and attended the same school. I quarterbacked our high school football team and Danny was the tailback. We were both drafted into the Army during the Korean War. When we got out of the service we joined the Fire Department together. We were as close as brothers.

After graduation from the academy we were assigned to Engine 27 in the Seventh Battalion. We established ourselves as pretty good firefighters. Danny soon developed a style that made him stand out among his peers. He was a rough tough nozzle man and would never leave until the fire was out. Once it was over he would walk out the front of the building and stand before the world like he had a spot light on him. He would raise his helmet in the air and extend his arms in a victory sign. He did this from day one until the day he retired. It was a Danny O'Brien trademark. We loved him for it.

Joe Barchilli was special people too. Joe won the medal of valor in 1976 for the rescue of an elderly lady trapped in a dwelling fire down in the Cass Corridor. Joe lost half an ear at that fire. The back draft, that occurred, burned off most of his hair. When it grew back it had a weird salt and pepper color. We used to kid Joe that his head looked like an ash tray. Every firefighter attending the wedding was a hero to some degree. They had served the city well. Many people were alive today because these guys were willing to make rescues that seemed impossible. Each had faced that heart pounding moment when experience and knowledge crosses into the realm of risk and uncertainty. It always amazed me how much punishment the human body can absorb when it is jacked up on adrenaline and focus.

Fire fighting is a risky business. You are taking a chance when you have to make a rescue alone. The odds of getting out safely are not good. Firefighting is a team activity. The urgency of the situation will sometimes make it necessary to move in without help. When you do there will be a knot in your gut as your mind runs through a list of options. Minutes feel like hours as the smoke thickens and the fire gets hotter. You know that you must find the victim before the super heated gases explode in a flashover. Most people killed in a fire are not victims of the flames. Smoke is the real assassin. Fire destroys and maims but smoke will kill in matter of minutes. You can feel the texture of the smoke change as you search for a victim. Raising a hand above your head will help gauge the heat of the fire. A rescuer must move quickly. As death crawls with you in a fire you become acutely aware that only the thin veneer of rubber in your mask is keeping you alive.

You must check the type of structure you are searching. A quick glance before entering will give you a thumbnail picture of the layout of the building. Time of day is important. If it is late at night you will search the bedrooms. In mid afternoon people will generally be on the first floor. Most important you must remember to protect your own life first. You must know when it is time to get out. If you go down other firefighters will be put at risk as they try to rescue you.

A fire scene can be a very chaotic place. Things happen fast. An axiom of the fire service is that when one thing turns to shit everything turns to shit. Mistakes tend to compound themselves and a small error can quickly become a major tragedy.

I once attended a Redmond Fire Safety Convention in Atlanta, Georgia. One of the lectures featured the Bradford Soccer Stadium fire in England. The film was cut from a television coverage tape. It was in real time and showed graphically how quickly a small fire can turn into a disaster. The soccer game was timed by a digital display on the TV screen which monitored the closing minutes of the contest. As the camera was following the action up and down the field it spotted a small rubbish fire in the stands. At the precise moment the fire is spotted the timer on the screen is at exactly zero. The timer shows the minute-by-minute progress of the unfolding tragedy. The astounding growth of the fire goes from a two by two area of burning paper and debris into an inferno that engulfs the entire grandstand. Within three minutes the small rubbish fire grew into a blaze that killed 56 people. The stadium was packed with spectators. Those who did not move quickly lost their lives. Those who ran down a stairway to the rear exit found the doors chained shut and perished beating on the door.

Responding fire companies arrived on the scene within three minutes. This is considered reasonable time in the fire service. The firefighters were powerless to affect a rescue. At the three minute point the fire's radiant heat was igniting the clothing and hair of persons fleeing across the soccer field. It was a total tragedy showing how fast events can become deadly at a fire. For many it meant going from eating popcorn to being dead in less than three minutes. This is the nature of fire.

Yes I was lucky to be here. My 30 year career was full of close calls. I had been involved in flashovers, back drafts, and building collapses. There were times when we responded to incidents that involved gunfire. Most notable was the civil disturbance in 1967. There were also the harrowing rides responding to fires.

I was once tillering the back end of Ladder 8 when the steering wheel snapped off. It happened as we swung around a corner. Only a quick reflex by the driver saved my life. He stopped Ladder 8 just short of going over the curb and rolling down a hill onto the freeway.

My friends attending the wedding had similar experiences. Looking back over thirty years I recalled numerous dangerous incidents involving this group of ex firefighters. The fire where Joe Barchilli lost half his ear was a good example.

It was one of those early morning fires. Joe and a man detailed in from another company were riding the back of Engine 31 that night. It was a busy night and all surrounding companies were working at fires. The nearest back up for Joe's company was Engine 37 that was approximately four miles away. To respond, Engine 37 would have to cross a busy section of railroad tracks.

Central office has the job of screening fire calls before dispatching a fire company to the scene. If an alarm box is pulled, central will send a full compliment of companies.

Typically you get three engines, one ladder truck, a squad and a chief. If a call comes in by phone, central office will determine what the response should be. On this night the fire was described as smoke coming from a rear window of a small dwelling. Central determined that a single company could handle the situation. They were wrong.

When Engine 31 arrived on the scene they found a two story flat totally involved in fire. People outside were yelling and waving their arms as Joe and his crew pulled up. Mac Pierce was in charge of Engine 31 that night. Mac thumbed his mike and reported to central that they had a working fire and would need help as soon as possible. Central alerted Engine 37 and sent a call to other more distant units. That's when things turned to shit.

The crew at Engine 37s quarters were in bed at 2 am but managed to get their rig on the road in less than a minute. They headed toward the fire down Dix Avenue with their siren wailing and flashers spinning. When they got to the tracks they were stopped by a slow moving freight train.

At the fire, Joe had taken the first line to the front of the building and started to spread out the hose so it would not kink. The detail man came running with the back up bundle. He tripped on the front walk and fell on a knee high iron fence that was topped by spikes. His kneecap was shattered. The injury rendered him useless. He went down screaming in agony. Mac Pierce yelled to his driver to help the injured man and sprinted to the fire to help Joe. The driver had hooked up to the hydrant and slammed in the pumps sending water to the fire. He then ran over to assist the injured man.

Joe opened the nozzle. He heard the distinctive sound of air moving ahead of the water. The open pipe gave a cough and a spit then blasted water against the front door of the dwelling. At this point a scream was heard from inside the building.

"There's someone in there. It sounds like they're trapped upstairs," Joe yelled.

It was a bad situation. There was no back up. They were all alone and had to act quickly. Entering a fully involved unventilated structure fire is a race with time. The choking yellow brown smoke can ignite a flashover at any moment.

"Here Mac take the line. I'm going in," Joe said.

Joe kicked open the door and they were buried in an avalanche of smoke and heat. Joe crawled in and the Captain Pierce remained at the door with a charged line.

"You got two minutes Joe and I'm coming in to get water on this fucking fire."

Up the stairs and down a hallway Joe scrambled. His neck and ears were singed by the heat. There was no visibility and Joe had to do everything by feeling with his hands. He decided to grope around in one more bedroom before he bailed out. He got lucky and felt the head and long hair of a person near a window. He was flat on his belly as he grabbed the victim's hair and started inching back toward the stairs. He knew he had only moments to get out before the flashover occurred. He was cutting it close. As he neared the stairs he discovered the victim was an elderly lady. He could feel the heat through his protective gear. He knew her skin may well be burning. He pulled off his helmet and jammed it over her unprotected face. The helmet insert with the Nomex ear flaps easily covered her head. After dragging her to the edge of the stairs, he was able to get her in a position to pick her up. It amazed him how much cooler it was two steps down the stairwell.

Joe was half way down the stairs and only steps from the outside door when the flashover happened. It blasted him head over heels into his captain who in that instant was able to open the charged line and cover them in a protective wall of water. They were out safely. Engine 37 arrived on the scene and firefighters were attacking the fire. The flashover had caught Joe on the side of his unprotected head. His hair was burned off and his left ear was cooked.

The old lady survived and Joe was awarded the Detroit Fire Department medal of valor for that year. His handsome black hair never returned. He got a thick growth of salt and pepper colored hair that looked like ashes. It was a small price to pay for saving a life. The guys used to kid him about his new hair color. They said he was only listening half the time with his left ear. I intended to kid him about those things at the wedding tonight.

As my wife Jo and I walked into the Knights of Columbus Hall I could hear a noisy group laughing and talking in the far corner of the room. The distinctive snort wheeze giggle of Tobin Barkley rose above the other laughter. They started yelling the moment they spotted us and it warmed my heart. These were the people I spent most of my working life with. It was like walking into an engine house when coming on duty. There were stories to be told and opinions to be wrestled with. It made me feel young again if only for a little while.

Tobin grabbed my hand in that big mitt of his and the other guys kissed and slobbered over my wife Jo. We hugged and laughed like a bunch of high school girls. It was going to be a great night. The room was full of happiness. As the evening wore on the guys would get a little outrageous but managed to stay in the bounds of propriety. After a few drinks the old tricks and high jinx appeared. A favorite trick, that always shocked people, was for the guys to kiss each other whenever the crowd would beat on their plates expecting the groom to smooch the bride.

Barkley loved to polka and he didn't care who he danced with. The ladies loved him. He was a powerful man with huge hands and size sixteen feet. I figured the gals did that association thing where big feet usually mean something else is big. At social affairs Tobin would have the girls lining up to dance with him.

The wedding was really starting to swing. The beer was cold and foamy, the shooters warm and tasty, and the music was loud and rocking the hall. Our wives were laughing and talking while the guys were rehashing old fires. Joe Bacilli's face was red and glowing. I could tell he was nearing his limit. Tobin Barkley was wheeling one of the gals around the floor to the beat of the Beer Barrel Polka. Every time he passed our group he would let out a yell or a whistle and stomp his feet. He was in his glory and at the top of his game

11

tonight. These were beautiful people. They had been through a lot together. They had earned this good time. The wedding provided the hall and this group was producing the fun.

Over the years we shared the joys and agonies of raising our families. When a big fire was burning the women called to comfort each other. We shared the sadness and gloom when we buried one of our own. Best of all we had a lot of good times and tons of laughter together.

Every year we took our kids downtown to see Santa come to town. We would meet at Engine 5 which was located near the starting point of the Thanksgiving Day Parade in Detroit. Firefighters and their families were invited for hot chocolate and cookies before and after the parade. The engine house would rock and roar with the laughter and giggles of the little kids. They all wanted to slide the pole or climb into the tiller seat of the ladder truck. It was a good time and we grew close as a fire department family. There were many other events that brought us together. We had the Firemen's Fund Field Day, Zoo Day, and the summer baseball tournament. We always had something going. It was fun. Firemen worked hard and they played hard. At the wedding our gang was going full tilt playing hard. Little did we know that our old adversary, fire, was planning another party tonight. It would be one we would never forget.

Chapter Three

Fire is a merciless killer that is difficult to contain. At the Training Academy we were taught that fire, like a triangle, has three sides. When fighting a fire you have to remove one or more of the sides of the triangle. When this is done the fire will be extinguished. Oxygen is one side of the triangle. Put a lid on a burning frying pan and you smother the fire by removing the oxygen.

Heat is the second side of the triangle. Get something hot enough and it will start to burn. Apply a spark to gasoline fumes and at you get an explosion of fire. Spontaneous combustion is a good example of a fire starting when enough heat is generated in something like oily rags.

Fuel is the last link in the triangle. In a fire almost everything is fuel. Fire will burn wood, plastic, the rugs, the wallpaper, the rubbish, the people, and even the firefighters. Fire will consume everything it can find and if you have the bad luck to be trapped in a burning building the fire will consume you.

Fire is man's friend when it is contained. We use it for heating, cooking, and in our industries to produce goods and products. We even use it when waging war to kill our enemies. We keep it contained in matches, cigarette lighters, furnaces, and bombs. All you have to do to bring it alive is connect the three sides of the triangle.

We have it contained and near us at all times. It is like having a pet tiger in your house. When fire gets out of control it becomes a deadly adversary. It will attack you and kill you. Firefighters are the Marines you call to battle an uncontrolled fire.

As we danced and sang the night away at the wedding, our old enemy, fire was preparing a surprise party at Cheboygan Community Hospital. The hospital was built in 1920. The facility contained outdated features including an unreliable sprinkler system. Safety devices now required by law for public buildings had not even been invented when the Community Hospital was built. Features like automatically closing doors to seal hallways in the event of fire, smoke alarms and fume detectors, pressurized rooms to keep smoke out, and adequate stairwell and door widths to accommodate movement out of the building were not included in the original construction. Hospital managers had installed some safety features but it was expensive. They decided to build a new structure instead. The new hospital was now under construction so updating anything in the old building had been put on hold

The rules and regulations required in public buildings have been established for a reason. Trying to evacuate patients from a burning hospital is one of the most difficult tasks a firefighter will face in his career. Buildings like, Cheboygan Community Hospital that lack safety devices make the job harder. Tonight firefighters would be tested by events that were starting to occur.

Smoking is prohibited in hospitals. If you want to smoke you must leave the building and go to an area designated for smokers. The man who was making a late delivery of bottled oxygen to the hospital needed a smoke. Wrestling the heavy green steel containers into the second basement of the hospital was exhausting work. The storage room was at the far end of a long hallway at the rear of the basement. Across from the storage room was a small alcove used for brooms, mops, and cleaning items. When he finished his delivery the young man slipped into the alcove closed the door and sat down. He reached into his shirt pocket and pulled out a pack of Marlboros. He knew there were no smoke detectors in this particular section of the building. He could smoke in safety here and have a relaxing break. Placing a lighted match to the tip of his cigarette he lit up and inhaled deeply. The warm tobacco flavored smoke slid into his mouth and deep into his lungs. He held his exhale for a moment then pursed his lips and blew a perfect smoke ring. There was nothing like enjoying a cigarette in the cozy confines of a private little room. The days of smoke breaks were over so a smoker had to improvise to enjoy a few moments with his pack of friends. He closed his eyes and puffed away.

He was half way through his cigarette when he heard footsteps pass over his head. Someone was moving in the first basement just above the room where he sat. Then the steel door at the head of the stairwell clanked open. If he was caught smoking in the hospital he could lose his job. Quickly he jammed the cigarette against the sole of his shoe. The crushed butt was then tossed into the corner where the mops were stored. He slipped out of the alcove and shut the door. He was moving down the hallway at a rapid pace when he encountered the night watchman making his rounds.

"Anyone else down here kid?" He was asked.

"Nope just me," he answered.

"Well come on I will walk you out and lock the doors."

They moved through the second basement, up to the first basement, then up to the first floor exit where the delivery truck was parked. The watchman slammed the door shut with a metallic clang. He secured a strong lock to prevent entry from the outside. The lock also prevented exit from the inside unless you had a key. This was against the fire code but who would know. The new hospital was in the process of being built so expensive safety features like new door locks had been ignored by the hospital administrators.

The discarded cigarette butt had landed on a dry mop head. Although crushed and smothered there remained a tiny ember alive and glowing. The compressed tobacco and paper slowly began to expand as it tried to regain its original form.

The crushing process bent the butt into a shape of a folded jack knife. Ever so slowly the butt opened and gasped for air. The alcove door had a small gap at floor level where oxygen flowed freely. The half bent cigarette sucked in the flowing air and began to glow again. The three sides of the fire triangle were now connected. The remaining spark of the cigarette was the heat, the tobacco and paper were the fuel, and the air near the floor supplied the oxygen. The fire was not under human control and could grow and consume as it saw fit.

The mop head was the first victim. Slowly it burned with a choking smoky stop start motion. More oxygen was needed and the fire crept up the wooden mop handle where it burst into a bright orange flame. The burning and heat caused the mop to fall from its leaning position and hit the floor. The handle bounced and hit an uncapped can of paint thinner stored near the wall. There was a whooshing sound as the fumes from the spilled container exploded in a fireball that filled the small room. In less than a minute the fire had expanded from a tiny amber in the cigarette to engulf the whole interior of the storage alcove. The oxygen was quickly consumed by the swirling banshee of hot flames as the fire searched frantically for more air. As the fire moved up the wall near a small sink it discovered a path out of the room. There were water pipes that went through the ceiling and the holes they passed through had not been sealed as the fire code required. The holes were an escape hatch for the growing fire. The pressure created by the expanding blaze shot bright yellow flames up the openings into the first basement storeroom. The store room was full of discarded cardboard boxes and used furniture. There were also several 50 gallon propane gas containers stored in a corner. They were used for the annual hospital barbeque. Staff members had been careless. They were supposed to put the gas tanks outside in the utility garage. In less than 30 seconds a second room was fully involved in fire. The flames continued to climb the wall and exploded like a geyser into the main floor linen room. The smoke and fire alarms sprang into action.

16

The watchman's control panel lit up with lights indicating there was a fire in the hospital.

As I said, when one thing turns to shit everything turns to shit. The events of the last two minutes proved that. A terrible price would be paid for the indiscretion of the careless smoker. The rules were there for a reason and he had ignored them. In his hurry to get rid of his cigarette, he failed to put it out completely. This was the first thing to go wrong. Second was the storage of the uncapped can of thinner that exploded when it was knocked over. Third was the code violation of not sealing the water pipes as they passed from floor to floor. The open pipe shafts allowed the fire to move at will. Things were out of control and firefighters were now needed.

Now a chance occurrence of fate came into play. Several hours earlier a fire had broken out at the State University which is located 50 miles south of Cheboygan. It started in a dormitory and fed by high winds spread quickly. There was a good chance it would involve the library adjacent to the dorm. The University Library contained a world-class collection of rare books. There were the papers and works of Ernest Hemingway on display in the lobby. The surrounding Fire departments responded but were losing the battle. The Governor, who was attending a reception at the school, intervened and made a snap decision. He ordered all fire protection in a 75 mile radius of the University to respond to the fire. Sending these units left a gaping hole in the blanket of fire protection for everyone in the 75 mile radius. The Cheboygan Fire Department and the volunteer support units were just arriving at the University when the fire broke out at the Cheboygan Community Hospital. To add to the series of screw ups was the fact that plumbers working on the hospital sprinkler system forgot to turn it on when they quit work that evening.

At the two minute point fire had extended to three floors. The flames in the alcove room not only spread upward but had rolled into the basement hallway. The flames tumbled and twisted to the stairway door and roared in protest at being confined. The combustibles on the next floor above the alcove were now burning with an angry intensity. The heat started to effect the propane tanks stored in the room. The gas cylinders were becoming explosive devices that could devastate this section of the hospital if they got hot enough. If you ever saw pictures of a napalm bomb exploding you will have a good mental image of what occurs when compressed propane blows up.

A fatal error was made by the watchman in the first minutes of the fire. When the alarm went off he got very excited. Bells were ringing and the control panel lights were flashing indicating the location of the fire. The activated alarm system automatically alerted the 911 operators but it was the watchman's job to verify the fire by phone. In his haste to check things out, the watchman forgot to make the call. The urgency of the situation could not be verified because of the missed call. The dispatcher decided to send a patrol car to investigate because all fire units had been sent to the State University.

Precious time was lost as the patrol car traveled the one mile from the police station to the hospital. At the three minute point the fire claimed its first victim. The watchman ran from his station down the front stairwell to the basement. He could see the haze of smoke at the far end of the building. What the hell was going on he thought, I was just down here less than fifteen minutes ago. He grabbed the handle of the steel door going down to the second basement. His last conscious act on earth was to jerk the door open. The fire in the closed off sub-basement was pressurized by the rolling black smoke and was gasping for more oxygen and fuel. The fire exploded out of the doorway like a leopard attacking a gazelle. In an instant it sank its smoky teeth into the watchman's Adams apple. The watchman's lungs bucked as he tried to get air. He half turned as the fire burned off his hair and clothes. He was charred and dead before he hit the floor. The ensuing flashover connected the fire with the flames on next level and the propane tanks in the storage room started to sizzle.

The patrol car pulled up to the entrance of the hospital. When Officer Kelly got out of the car he could smell smoke. It was late and visiting hours were over so the parking lot was relatively empty. He trotted into the building and turned right to enter the watch station. He could see nurses and attendants scurrying around the hall as they began to implement fire drill procedures.

"Where the hell is the watchman?" He muttered to himself.

He stepped back into the hall and young nurse's aide crashed into him. They both went sprawling on the floor. People were heading for the exits. He could hear yelling from the far end of the building. The fire had moved quickly. The acrid smell of smoke permeated the air. Heat was beginning to accumulate and move with the expanding blaze. He heard the heart stopping screams of someone shouting fire.

Human beings have been developing the process of communication for millions of years. Certain words mean different things. The way a word is spoken, its tone, or volume can send different messages. There is an unmistakable sole chilling sound when a person is in a panic. A person screaming fire in a high-pitched voice will quickly infect others with the panic reaction. Panic diminishes the ability to reason things out. It pushes the body into a survival mode. The response is usually to run as adrenaline is poured into the blood stream. Adrenaline will give an individual added strength, sometimes even superhuman strength. Tonight panic ruled the halls of Cheboygan Community Hospital.

Officer Jim Kelly could feel that tell tale tickle in his gut as his body started to prepare for action. His senses keened as the fight or run reaction entered his brain. He was a trained professional. He had learned to harness the power of adrenaline to help him do his job. Firefighters and emergency personnel react in the same way. That is why they seem to be so cool under fire. Believe me when I say the appearance is deceiving. In dangerous situations, emergency workers are constantly suppressing the urge to leave. A nurse trying to stop the flow of blood in a hemorrhaging accident victim or a police officer facing down an armed killer must keep cool to do their job. On this evening Jim Kelly knew his next actions meant life or death for the people in this building.

Chapter Four

Molly Means was the on duty nurse working the intensive care unit that night. There were six children in her care. One was a toddler recovering from pneumonia and five children were recovering from various surgeries. At this hospital the normal patient to nurse ratio in the IC unit was three to one. Because the staff was stretched thin, Molly was working alone.

She looked at the clock when the fire alarm went off. It was 10:30 pm. Hospital protocol required her to close the fire resistant door that sealed the IC unit from the hallway. Next she prepared the patients to be moved. Some of the kids were hooked up to IVs and attached to monitoring devices. Molly double checked the vital signs and condition of each child as she prepared them for movement. Lulu the toddler started to cry when the activity disturbed her sleep. She was a precious little girl with big round blue eyes, curly blond hair, and skinny legs. Molly just loved to hold and cuddle her. The kids asked Molly what was going on. Molly calmed them and told them it was probably just another fire drill.

Molly's heart skipped a beat when she looked out the window of the room. She could see groups of hospital patients and hospital personnel gathering in the designated fire drill area. They were looking at the rear of the building where she was located. A police car with flashers still spinning was parked near the front door. Looking up Main Street, she saw another police car responding. She asked herself, "Where are the fire engines?" Her blood ran cold when she saw the first wisps of smoke pass by the window. This was the real thing. She felt butterflies in her stomach as she realized the gravity of her situation.

The first responding officer, Jim Kelly, sprang into action as he scrambled to his feet. The collision with the fleeing nurse's aide had stunned him momentarily. Others were hastily rushing out the door as Kelly keyed his portable radio.

"Send help. There is a working fire at the Community Hospital. We need as many emergency personnel as you can find."

"How bad is the fire?" The dispatcher asked.

"We have the makings of a goddamn disaster happening here. Get some people up here and do it now."

"I read you but there are no fire units available. The entire department is out of town working at the University fire. I will send additional police to assist you."

"I need firemen not cops."

"Copy that," replied the dispatcher.

Molly had determined that the kids could be put in wheel chairs or carried if necessary. None of them were in bad shape. The healing power of the young is amazing. These kids were well on the way to recovery and Molly was sure they would manage an evacuation with ease. The excitement of the fire had turned the children into chatter boxes. They started to ask Molly questions.

"Are we going to die Molly?"

"Are the fire engines coming?"

"Can we bring our toys?"

Molly told them, "We must be quiet. I want you to do what I tell you. I promise you all a treat when this is over. Do you hear me?"

"Yes Molly," the children answered in unison.

We are in deep trouble if this fire extends to my floor, Molly thought. I'm going to have to think about how I will move six children alone. Again she wondered where are the firefighters? The kids began coughing and Lulu started crying in earnest as smoke slowly seeped into the room.

Officer Jim Kelly met the arriving patrol car at the front of the building. His plan of action was to search the hospital and evacuate any remaining patients. He would need one of the responding police officers to help him. The other he would send back to town to get more help. Kelly was now aware there were no fire units available to respond.

His confidence was bolstered when he saw police officers Chum Dupree and his brother Mel running up the front steps. These were two tough cops. Both were Viet Nam veterans. They were ex marines and Mel had earned a Navy Cross at Khe San.

Kelly yelled to Chum, "Get back to town and get more men. Mel and I will do what we can until you get back."

As he ran out the door Chum yelled, "I'm going straight to the Knights of Columbus Hall. Someone told me there will be a lot of firefighters attending the wedding tonight. Maybe they can help."

"Good thinking Chum but those firefighters are old geezers. They may be more of a hindrance than a help."

"I'll get them up here anyway. I'll pass by the high school and see if I can scratch up any more bodies. The football team is supposed to meet in the gym this evening"

Officer Kelly turned to Mel and said, "Let's think this out before we move. We know the fire is located at the back of the building. We know the watchman is gone. We know there are no firefighters responding and chances are we are going to lose the entire building."

"Well the only thing we can do is try to get everyone out and we better get cracking," Mel answered.

"Ok. Let's stick together in case we have to carry someone out. Come on let's start as close to the fire as we can get."

The two men ran toward the rear of the hospital as the gathering smoke forced them into a crouching position.

Each corridor in the building was divided into three sections. Each section has a door separating it from the adjacent section. The closing off of rooms and hallways is designed to impede the progress of any fire that may occur. Fire will follow the path of least resistance and open doors are the routes it generally uses. In an ideal situation the fire doors will compartmentalize the blaze so a working sprinkler system can contain it until the Fire Department arrives to extinguish the flames. What was happening this evening was not an ideal situation. The sprinkler system was not working and there were no responding firefighters.

Officer Kelly knew that the elevators were automatically shut down when the fire alarm was engaged. Elevator shafts become chimneys during a fire. The elevator can become a death cage for those trapped inside. The watchman carries an elevator key. He will give it to trained professional firefighters to operate the elevators in emergency situations. The watchman had disappeared so Kelly and Mel would have to use the stairs to make a search of the building.

They started at the first fire door. As they slipped into the hallway they encountered thickening smoke. They proceeded to the next fire door and peered through the fire proof glass window. They could see flames had filled the corridor. The fire was rampaging in this section of the hospital. Kelly knew that anyone who remained in that hallway was now dead. It was reasonable to think that those people still on the upper floors were in grave danger. They started to hear the cooking propane tanks.

"Man this fire looks bad. Can you hear that high-pitched whistling sound? Kelly asked.

"Yeah I hear it. I wonder what it is."

They both turned and headed for the enclosed stairwell.

The propane tanks in the first floor storage room were intended for use on the barbeque burner. The fire was rapidly turning them into deadly bombs. Pressurized propane gas will expand when heated. The steel container will rupture if it gets hot enough. The escaping gas will ignite in a fearsome explosion. The whistling sound the police officers were hearing was a warning that the propane tanks were about to blow.

Kelly and Mel bounded up the stairwell taking two and three steps at a time. They hit the second floor and popped the door open. They hurried down the hallway looking into each room as they proceeded. The smoke was rapidly filling the hallway and they could feel the temperature rising. They moved past the last fire door that separated the hall into three sections. As they moved they could hear a louder high-pitched whistling sound coming from the rear of the building. They were drenched in sweat and their hearts were pounding.

Mel shouted, "No one is here Jim."

"Looks like they all got out. Let's check the third floor before the fire gets there. You know Mel that goddamn screeching sound is starting to scare the hell out of me."

"Yeah me to," Mel replied.

It happened as they turned to leave. There was a deafening roar as the first tank exploded. The second tank was driven through the concrete wall near the ceiling. It soared into the air in a graceful arc. At the apex of its trajectory it detonated. The fireball was fifty feet wide. A magnificent red, white, and orange flash lit the night sky like a giant Fourth of July rocket. A shower of steel shards came down close to where the people who had evacuated the building were standing.

The blast blew out the supporting wall of the second floor. The rear of the building sagged as the top floors pan caked down one level to fill the void. Tons of debris showered down on the two police officers. They were knocked to the floor by the concussion. The power of the explosion pushed fire in every direction. Flames shot over their heads and the heat scorched their ears and necks. It was hard to breathe as the mixture of smoke and dust settled around them.

Coughing and gasping, Kelly yelled for his partner, "You alright Mel?"

He only heard groans for a reply. Quickly he dug himself out of a pile of collapsed ceiling drywall and assorted timbers. As he stood up he banged his head on the floor joists of the caved in third floor. They were in a confined space approximately four foot high. It was completely dark. Kelly snapped on his flashlight and scanned the area. A few feet behind him he could see Mel's arm protruding from a pile of ruble. Crawling closer he could make out Mel's head and shoulders. The rest of Mel's body was buried in the ungodly mess of the pulverized building. Kelly knelt over his partner. He brushed the fallen plaster from his face.

"How you doing pal?" He asked.

"I feel like shit and I can't move my legs. There is crap around them and it feels like my ankle is in a bear trap or something."

Kelly moved the beam of his flashlight around the area. He could see they were entombed in a small space about 15 feet long by four feet wide. There was only enough head room to move in a crouching position. It was a bad situation. The initial blast had shot the fire outward. The resulting vacuum had sucked the flames back so there was a momentary reprieve as the fire prepared to expand again.

Kelly activated his radio to call for help. He sent his message, "Two officers down. We are trapped somewhere on the third floor. The building has collapsed and we need help now."

The dispatcher answered, "I read you. We will get you help as soon as possible. You are priority one for all responders. Are you injured?"

"No. But my partner is half buried and we need help immediately."

The ceiling groaned and made a screeching sound as it settled another two inches over their heads. With the temperature rising, Kelly realized they were trapped in a make shift oven.

Mel looked up at Kelly and said, 'Well the good news is the damn whistling noise finally stopped."

26

Kelly chuckled. He was thinking what a tough bastard his partner was. Here they were probably facing the last minutes of there lives and this guy is making jokes. He started digging vigorously to free his friend.

Molly Means was really frightened now. The blast had knocked her down. The collapse had sent carts and portable monitoring devices hurtling around the room. A heart monitor had smashed into Molly's leg and blood oozed from a large gash. The children were screaming in fear as Molly huddled them around her. She checked them and found no injuries. Molly knew they had to get out of there before things got worse.

The wall phone in the IC unit was dead. Molly pulled a cell phone out of her pocket and dialed 911. The answer came immediately, "What is your emergency please?"

"There is a fire at the Community Hospital. We are trapped on the fifth floor in the intensive care room. Please help us."

"How many of you are there. Do you have injuries?"

"No injuries but I have six small kids with me. Please hurry. We are scared."

"Stay where you are. Help is on the way."

Officer Chum Dupree stopped at the high school. Only one person remained after the late night football meeting was over. It was Billy Svenson the star fullback of the Cheboygan Chiefs.

"Get in Billy I need your help," yelled Chum.

"What's going on Officer Dupree?"

"There's a fire at the hospital and we need help to get people out of the building."

"Holy crap my sister Lulu is there with pneumonia. Let's go."

Billy was still closing the door of the patrol car when Chum slammed the gas pedal to the floor. The wheels spun and showered the gymnasium wall with cinders and stones. The car swerved and yawed as it tried to get traction. The tires caught and the police car hurtled toward the street. Chum turned the siren on full blast. He wanted to attract as much attention as possible. Lights were going on all over town and dogs were barking. The explosion and sirens were turning everyone out to see what was going on. Chum hoped they could muster a fire fighting crew from the people headed for the hospital.

He turned into the Knights of Columbus parking lot on two wheels. The patrol car skidded sideways again and almost spun out. Chum got control and sped up to the front door. He and Billy left the car doors open as they bounded into the building. Chum ran directly to the stage where the disc jockey was playing music for the wedding. He picked up the microphone and looked at the crowd. He saw the bride and groom had already departed. Only friends and relatives remained. God I hope these people are in shape to help me tonight he thought.

When Chum put the mike near his mouth it screeched an electronic protest. That seemed to get everyone's attention. He pulled back a little and tapped the mike with a thump thump sound.

"May I have your attention please," he began.

The talking, shuffling, and sounds of glass tinkling stopped. All faces were turned toward Chum. A police officer at the microphone meant something serious was happening. The room became attentive as the crowd waited for officer Dupree to speak.

He said, "There is a fire at the Community Hospital. The governor has called all our fire protection to a fire at the University. Our firefighters are out of town working at that fire. We need every person who thinks they can help to report to the hospital. I understand there is a group of Detroit firefighters here tonight. Could that group please meet me at the front door of the hall?" The rest of you, who can help, please go immediately to the hospital.

There was stunned silence for a moment before the hall erupted in action. People were grabbing their things and heading for the exits. Car doors were slamming and the peeling of tires could be heard as the first helpers headed for the hospital. The retired firefighters were gathered by a table near the front door.

"God damn it. I knew something was wrong when I went out for a smoke. I saw the sky light up and heard a boom. I thought it was some sort of fireworks but the boom sounded like that tanker that went up at Marathon Oil in 1985,"Danny O'Brien said.

Experienced firefighters are super sensitive to sounds and smells. Over the years they develop a sixth sense when events are occurring at the scene of emergencies. Danny identified the boom as threatening because he remembered the sound of the explosion at the refinery. That blast had killed five workers and became a dangerous fifth alarm. Before this night was out the senses and abilities of Danny and his friends would be severely tested. We gathered around officer Dupree and listened intently.

"This is the situation as we know it," he said. "We have an out of control fire at Cheboygan Community Hospital. My dispatcher has just informed me that my brother and his partner are trapped in the building somewhere on the third floor. There is a nurse and six kids holed up in the IC unit on the top floor waiting for help. There has been an explosion that caused a partial collapse of the building. All fire protection is out of the city. There will be no help coming for at least an hour. By then it will be too late. You are the only trained firefighters in Cheboygan and we need your help. Can you do it?"

Tobin Barkley answered for all of us, "Damn right we'll help but we have no rig or tools."

Chum said, "Let's get down to the Fire station. I know there is extra gear there and probably some back up fire apparatus. We have to go now or we will lose those people at the hospital."

Billy Svenson added a plea, "Please hurry. My sister Lulu is supposed to be in the intensive care room."

Joe Barcilli gave Billy a hard look and said, "Look kid, we used to be firefighters. We aren't even a shadow of what

29

we used to be. We are going to try to get those people out but don't get your hopes up."

Joe looked at us and shook his head.

"It looks like it is going to be a long night. We better get going."

We left the wedding and piled into two cars to follow officer Dupree to the fire station.

Chapter Five

We arrived at the fire hall minutes after we left the wedding. I watched as each man walked into the building. There was Joe Barchilli, Mac Pierce, Tobin Barkley, Bobby Kazoo, Danny O'Brien, Benny Borza, Carl Bolden and me Bob Haig. This was truly an over the hill gang. Each of us had some degree of disability. Barcilli's bad hip was probably the worst. It caused Joe to walk with a noticeable limp. My hands could not sustain a strong grip anymore because they were broken in an accident while responding to a fire. Carl had a bad liver from a chemical fire. The rest of them were damaged goods. We had given everything we had to the Fire Department. Many people were alive today because of our efforts. We were not sure we were up to the task ahead but we were sure as hell going to give it our best shot.

Each of us had risen in the Department to the rank of Captain or Chief. The challenge we faced tonight would draw on our years of experience. We would need all the knowledge we possessed, plus every ounce of luck that providence could provide. Sometimes you have to rely on luck. There are times when you must take a chance and gamble. Those of us in that Cheboygan Fire Hall had been winners most of our careers. We had buried many of our comrades who were not so lucky. So here we were, ready to challenge our old enemy, fire. Would our luck hold out? We were going to find out shortly.

Joe was our leader. He was the acknowledged best firefighter among us.

He barked orders, "Bobby, start checking out those two rigs to see if they run. The rest of you guys find some turnout gear and air tanks. We are going to need a lot of air tonight so bring all the extra bottles you can find."

We split up to scour the rooms for equipment. The locker room produced helmets, boots, and coats. This department was a mix of professionals and volunteers so there was an excess of equipment. We found self-contained breathing apparatus and spare tanks in a storage area next to the locker room. Bobby fired up the diesel engine on the X-rig. I got a shot of adrenalin as I heard the throaty roar fill the room. We were going on a run again to face another fire. In all the years I spent on the department I never failed to get a case of the butterflies when we went on a run.

Bobby Kazoo had the ancient Seagrave J-model purring in a soft grumbling idle when he crossed the apparatus room floor to check out the other rig. He started to laugh when he looked at the old Arhens Fox pumper. It was a 1920s vintage fire engine. It was in mint condition and shined like the buttons on an honor guard's uniform. It had a large wooden steering wheel that protruded straight up from the floorboard. It was an open rig and had a distinctive large chrome ball in front of the engine. There were large bars, handgrips and controls next to the driver's seat. A huge bell sat just in front of the chrome pressure ball. The flasher lights sat on top of a pole next to the Captain's seat. The lights rotated like a child's toy pinwheel when activated. The rig was older than all of us and in much better shape. You could tell the volunteers had babied this old Arhens Fox. It was probably a center piece for any parade they participated in. She was going to war again if Bobby could figure out how to start. her. He found a crank under the front seat and tossed it to Danny O'Brien.

"Start cranking Danny," he yelled.

Bobby jumped into the driver's seat. He gave a quick glance at the control gauges and turned on the starter switch. Danny gave several hard cranks before the old rig backfired, belched smoke, and started. The crank kicked back and knocked Danny on his ass. Danny cursed. A few more backfires and the rig started to purr. The engine house sounded like the flight deck of an aircraft carrier as both engines started to hum in unison.

"Ready to go Joe," Bobby shouted.

"Ok guys let's do it. Stay close and look for a hydrant when we get to the scene. Assemble on me when we get there," Joe directed.

Lee Long and Carl Bolden opened the engine house doors. Benny Borza climbed behind the wheel of the Seagrave J-model and gave a quick scan of the controls. Bobby Kazoo said he would drive the Arhens Fox because it might require a little more expertise. Both drivers looked back to check their riders. The J-model was an enclosed fire truck where the passengers rode in the rear next to the hose bed. The Arhens Fox was a little more dangerous to ride because the firefighters had to hang onto the sides or stand on a narrow rear running board. Present day firefighters must be seated and strapped in with a safety belt as prescribed by OSHA regulations. The flamboyant cowboy style of riding a rig has been outlawed. The safety rules are necessary and have saved lives. Tonight we were cowboys and we were hanging all over those rigs as they started to roll.

Bolden and Long slammed the engine house doors and ran to the moving apparatus.

Before Bolden got on the J-model he grabbed Billy Svenson by the arm and yelled in his ear, "Come with us. We are going to need your muscles. Get in the back of the rig and put on some of that fire gear."

Billy motioned to officer Dupree that he would be riding with us and jumped into the back of the J-model. The patrol car flashers and siren were turned on and we were on our way to the Community Hospital.

As we turned on to Main Street we could see the telltale glow in the sky. The fire had vented out the rear of the building after the explosion occurred. Bright yellow orange flames reached skyward as they sucked the oxygen out of the fall air. The fire rolled and twisted as it belched black brown smoke indicating it was feeding on fuel. The fire monster was growing like a genie let out of a bottle. The three sides of the fire triangle harmonized in a deadly song.

Bolden, Lee Long, Billy Svenson and I were riding in the back of the J-model. Benny Borza was driving with Joe Barchilli sitting in the boss's seat manning the radio. We were helping Billy into his turnout gear. We gave him instructions on how to use the self-contained breathing apparatus.

Bolden told Billy, "When we get to the fire, I want you to stick to me like glue. You are my responsibility and we must work as a team. We will need your strength for the job ahead."

"Yes sir but can we look for my sister first when we get there?"

"We will look for her as soon as we can. I promise."

I was glad that Bolden was going to watch out for the kid. Bolden was a top notch squad man. He had earned his spurs early by working in busy fire companies. They always assigned the trial firefighters to Bolden's care. He had a knack for calming the anxieties of rookies facing their first fire. He earned that trust by his actions at a fire down in the Seventh Battalion one night.

It was an early morning blaze in a commercial building that had been cooking for sometime. It was a smoky one. Bolden and his trial man were on the pipe inching their way across a room searching for the seat of the fire. There was zero visibility because rolling brown smoke filled the building from floor to ceiling. They had moved about 30 feet across what appeared to be a show room floor. The trial man had the nozzle with Bolden right next to him with an arm around his waist. They were crawling on their hands and knees to stay below the tremendous heat build up above their heads. Bolden had his face close to the trial man's ear and was talking him through the fire.

"You're going to be all right. You are doing fine. Keep the nozzle on fog and keep moving. You will see a flash of flame in the smoke when we hit the fire. When that happens we will move in and kill it."

Bolden stayed close to his trial firefighter. He knew that human contact is reassuring when death and destruction is raging around you in a gown of hot smoke.

The hot floor started to burn their knees. Bolden realized too late that the fire was located in the basement directly below them. There was a sickening cracking sound as the floor gave way. Suddenly Carl Bolden was alone. The trial man was gone. He had dropped into the basement where the fire had originated. Bolden could hear his panicked calls for help.

"Don't move kid and don't take your mask off. I will get you out," Bolden promised.

Suddenly a hand touched his back. It was Danny O'Brien who had followed the line in with the intent of relieving the pipe man.

"God I'm glad you're here Danny. I got my trial man down in the basement and we are going to need help to get him out."

There were no hand held radios in those days so all communication was verbal. They could not call others to their aid.

Bolden told Danny, "Go back and tell the Captain what's happening and bring the Dutch Town ladder back in here. I'm going to stay with the kid."

The dutch town is a short ladder that Bolden intended to lower into the basement to rescue the trial man. Danny turned and followed the hose line out the door.

"Be back in a minute," he shouted.

Bolden sat on the floor and swung his legs into the gapping hole with his feet dangling in the hole, Bolden used the hose line like a rope to lowered himself into the basement. He had to be careful not to snag his air tank on the jagged pieces of wood as he moved downward. With this move he was risking his life. There was no way a firefighter in full gear could climb back up that line. It was now put out the fire or die. The only other option was for Danny to come back with that ladder to bail them out of the jam they were in.

The trial man was breathing heavily. He was sucking so hard on his mask that he sounded like a kid draining the bottom of a soda glass.

"Calm down kid. We can do this. Keep your cool and hand me that nozzle you are laying on," Bolden said.

It was hotter than hell down there and the sound of the trial man's warning bell meant he only had five minutes of air left in his tank. Bolden prayed Danny would get back in time.

The fire was rolling around their heads. It was trying to move up through the hole the kid created when he fell through. Bolden huddled over his trial man and turned the nozzle to full fog. He whipped the pipe back and forth in a circular motion above their heads. He was not winning the fight but he wasn't losing either. As he and the rookie clung together they could hear movement on the floor above them.

"Hey you guys still down there?" Danny shouted.

"Yes you asshole. We are still down here. Where did you think we would be, at Casey's? Get us the hell out of here. We're burning up," Bolden yelled.

Danny lowered the ladder and they were up and out quickly. When they moved out the front door they could see and hear additional companies arriving on the scene. With the successful rescue of his buddy and the trial man Danny celebrated by lifting his helmet into the air and raising his arms in a victory sign. Bolden just smiled and shook his head. The fire went to five alarms and eventually destroyed the building before it was brought under control. Both the trial man and Bolden received miner burns but lived to fight another day. This was an example of the type of firefighter Carl Bolden was. He had been willing to sacrifice his life to save his partner. Yes Billy Svenson was in good hands.

In a Seagrave J-model the driver's cab and the back of the rig are separated by a partition with a small sliding window. There is a seat sitting back to back with the front cab where firefighters can sit on the way to a fire. There is a passage way between two hose beds used for exit and entry. Additional firefighters can ride in this space. This is how we were riding the rig on the way to the fire. We were trying to see the burning hospital through the front window of the fire engine as we raced down Main Street.

Joe Barchilli turned on the rig radio and identified himself to the dispatcher. "This is KQA the Detroit Fire Department responding to Cheboygan Community Hospital," he reported.

There was stunned silence for a moment and the 911 operator came back with, "Please clarify your message."

Joe responded, "We are a group of Detroit Firefighters en route to the fire. We have been recruited by the local Police Department. We have two apparatus taken from the fire station. We are geared and ready to go. Can you give us a status report on the fire?"

"You have a working fire at the hospital. You will be the only firefighters on the scene. There are two police officers trapped on the second or third floor. Calls indicate there are a nurse and children in trouble on the fifth floor. The fire has trapped them in the intensive care unit. We have no report from the night watchman and assume he is missing also. All fire units are working out of town. You can expect no help for at least an hour."

"Read you loud and clear. Thanks for the report. I will contact you by the police prep radio when we begin our attack on the fire," Joe answered.

The window between the front and back of the rig was open so we all heard the report. Joe turned and asked, "You guys have any comments or suggestions?"

"Joe, I think we should concentrate on getting the people out of the building. Especially those kids," I offered.

Joe said, "I agree but we have to get some water on that fire to buy us time. We have to stop it in its tracks if we can.

We will split into three teams. Danny O'Brien, Tobin Barkley and Mac Pierce will attack the fire with the first hose line. Bob Haig you and I will take Bolden and the kid to make an attempt to get up to the fifth floor. If we make it, there may be a chance to save them. Borza and Lee Long will search for those trapped cops. They can take the cop who recruited us along with them."

Lee Long asked, "What about communications Joe?"

"We only have one radio so we will let the cop rescue team have it. They may be able to talk to the trapped guys."

Our battle plan was set when arrived on the scene. As we pulled into the parking lot we could see a crowd had gathered. They were cheering and shouting as we pulled up. It reminded me of my high school days when we came out of the tunnel at the state championship football game. We bounced out of the J-model rig in full battle gear. We had our game faces on. We were determined to win this battle and we damn sure knew it was no game.

Bobby Kazoo spotted a hydrant about a hundred feet from the building. Fire Engine Operators had to be careful where they positioned their pumpers. More than one rig had been lost when hooked up too close to a burning building. I can remember the first time I saw that happen.

It was an extra alarm fire at the abandoned Central Train Station near downtown Detroit. We arrived on third alarm with Engine 27. We worked a large two and a half inch line into the building. Other companies were doing the same thing all along the front of the train station. We snaked the bulky hose through several hallways and out onto a platform near the back of the station. It was hot and smoky. I was with Mac Pierce and a detail man from an east side company.

The building was several blocks long and totally in-volved. It had been an abandoned boarded up hulk for years. Most likely some homeless people had made it into a hobo hotel. Homeless people would build a fire to stay warm in these derelict structures. Left unattended the fire could get out of control and grow to a conflagration like the one we were now battling.

Lines were taken into the old train station at various entrances along the front of the 300 foot long building. Engine 13 put first water on the fire and was hooked up to a hydrant about 50 feet from the main entrance. It worked out to be a poor choice of hydrants. Everyone was using big water. The smaller inch and a half bundles could be seen strewn along the street in front of the blazing building. They would be used later in the clean up when the fire was over.

We were making good progress. Each fire team rolled back the fire in their area of attack. We had reclaimed about half of the 100 foot wide building. Like my crew the others could see the rear platform, the tracks, and an open area that extended to the Detroit River.

Out of the corner of my eye I could see the fire boat heeling over as it turned and started for a run on the train station. This can't be happening I thought. A rule in the Department was to never shoot water into a building when firefighters are working inside. As the boat came close to the shore line it turned up river and slowed. All water cannons were trained on the fire. Apparently the Chief working this fire had forgot the rules of engagement.

A fire boat can deliver a tremendous volume of water onto a fire. To my disbelief the water cannons opened all at once. It looked like the Battleship Missouri firing a salvo on D Day. The results were disastrous. The enormous volume of water created a wall of pressure that reversed the fire and created a rolling ball of flame and heat. We only had seconds to drop our lines and head back toward the street. We were running blindly in the smoke. We were being chased by a tidal wave of fire. Our only chance was to follow the hose line out. We had thrown off our heavy air bottles like fighter planes dropping their wing tanks.

It was a run for our lives. About half way out, the last hallway took a quick turn to the left before it straightened out to lead to the front door. Mac Pierce was leading the way. We were running in a crouching position trying to not lose sight of the hose line. I was at the rear of our group and could feel the pressure on my back as the fire ball picked up speed. It was making a whooshing snorting sound like a charging wild boar. I was yelling to hurry. Other escaping firefighters could be heard shouting as they attempted to flee the roaring flames. Mac forgot about the sharp left turn and in his haste crashed into the wall. He bounced back and we pancaked into each other in a violent collision. Mac was up first. He grabbed me and the detail by our collars and pulled us around the bend of the corridor. The fire ball smacked into the wall and hesitated giving us a momentary reprieve. We scrambled to our feet and ran the last thirty feet to the doorway. The fire caught us in midair as we leaped off the front loading dock. We were singed, dirty and snot was hanging in long slimy strings from our noses but we were alive and safe.

I looked down the length of the block long building and saw firefighters being ejected from doorways like popcorn from an open cooker. Many of them had steam and smoke coming off their bodies. It was a miracle that we got out safely.

I could see Engine 13 light up in flames as the fire ball rolled over the rig. The engineer jumped into the driver's seat and tried to back the pumper away from the fire plug. The soft suction was still attached to the hydrant making it impossible to back away. The engineer had to jump out and run for his life. It was a hard lesson for everyone. It reinforced the rule of being sure you to always hook up a safe distance from a fire. Tonight Bobby Kazoo was following that rule because he had been the driver of Engine 13 on that fateful night. Lessons learned the hard way are not easily forgotten.

Chapter Six

Bobby Kazoo positioned the ancient Arhens Fox to one side of the hydrant. Joe ordered Borza to back the J-model to a doorway at the side of the burning hospital. The read on the fire said it had started either in the first or second basement. The rear area was totally involved. Heavy smoke was pouring out the lower windows and roaring flames were licking up the back wall. We could see a sag in the center rear area where the explosion caused the collapse. Heavy duty electric wires came into the hospital from a power station near our attack site. The fire burned off several of the wires and they had dropped to the ground. They were bouncing and spitting sparks like a lion tamer's whip. Joe called the dispatcher requesting the power company be sent to the scene.

Bobby Kazoo was out of his rig at the hydrant screwing off the caps. He attached the hydrant wrench to the top of the fire plug. He quickly attached the hydrant gate to one of the openings and checked to see if the valve was closed. The gate is used to hook up a second pumper to the same hydrant. Bobby turned and looked toward the fire.

Borza turned his rig and prepared for a run to the hydrant where Bobby Kazoo waited anxiously. Men were at the rear of the rig pulling the line off both hose beds. Everyone was working now. The police car pulled close and officer Dupree ran to assist the firefighters setting up for the initial attack on the fire.

Joe barked out the orders, "Officer, you take the rescue team to where you last saw your partners. Try to contact them with your prep radio. Inform the dispatcher that we are starting to attack the situation at three points. Danny, Barkley and Mac Pierce will attack the fire and try to push it toward the back of the building. Lee Long and Borza will go with you to get your guys out. The rest of us are going to attempt to find those kids. Those of you without air tanks get one on. Be sure to take an extra tank with you."

We were geared and ready to go. I thought about how those fire horses would shiver in anticipation before the action started. That was us, a bunch of old fire horses.

Fire fighting is a dangerous violent occupation. It requires strength, courage, and quick thinking. The stakes are high. Firefighters called to an emergency must handle the situation. There is no one else to call. Time is of the essence and in many cases lives are at stake. A fire will grow at an exponential rate. It doubles in size every sixty seconds. We were waiting for Bobby Kazoo to send us water so we could begin to battle this fire to stop it in its tracks.

With a loud roar the J-model took off for the hydrant. An engine dropping line on a run to a hydrant is a graceful sight to behold. The 1500 feet of two and a half inch hose stacked neatly in the bed of the truck starts to unload. It peels off the truck like a harpoon shot from a Whaler's gun. There is a swishing noise as each length of hose takes a dive for the street. The thump clunk sound of the two and a half inch line hitting the ground is interspersed with the occasional clank of the brass hose connections bouncing off the pavement. Like a giant red spider the engine leaves a trail of hose as it moves to connect a water source to the men working at the fire.

Bobby Kazoo was waiting as Borza nosed the rig close to the hydrant. Before the J-model stopped, he pulled the soft suction off the front of the rig. In seconds he made the connection. The soft suction acts like a giant straw that pulls water from the hydrant into the pumps of the engine. As water passes through the engine pumps, pressure is applied and it is sent to the firefighters manning the nozzles.

Borza placed the apparatus in pumping mode and jumped out of the cab. He hurried to the rear of the rig and disconnected the brass butt from the line he had just stretched from the fire. He hooked the line to the opening connector near the control panel and gave Bobby Kazoo the thumbs up sign. Bobby grabbed the hydrant wrench attached to the opening nut on the hydrant and spun it open. Water rushed up to the hydrant from the water main buried far below and passed into the pumps of the waiting engine. Bobby moved like a cat to the controls on the side of the rig. He adjusted the pressure and opened the gate to charge the line with water.

It was over a hundred feet to the burning building. Borza was moving as fast as his old body would allow. He was already sweating profusely. I'm running out of gas and I haven't even got to the fire he thought. He heard the hissing sound of the air moving in front of the water as it filled the hose. He was following the line back to the fire. He watched as the hose filled, straightened, and hardened up. He grinned. It reminded him of the powerful erections he had as a teenager.

Everything was going smoothly to this point. The men had pulled off enough extra line to move deep into the building. Danny was on the nozzle in a kneeling position putting on his mask. The others were spreading out the hose line in a zig zag pattern so there would be no kinks to slow the flow of water. There was a momentary lull as we waited for the water to arrive. We looked at each other and started to grin. Barkley was the first to laugh. He started with that snort wheeze giggle of his and then broke into a robust hee haw belly laugh. Soon all of us except the cop and Billy were roaring.

"Isn't this some bullshit. None of us have the strength to screw our old ladies anymore and we are about to take on this bastard fire," Danny blurted out between giggles.

Barkley had to lift the face piece of his mask to wipe the laughter tears from his face.

He said, "Yeah we are a bunch of ass holes but you know what? I'm excited."

Joe was still grinning when he said, "OK guys let's get ready. We are into some serious crap here and we better keep our wits about us."

He put his arms around Borza and Lee Long and gave them a hug..

"You guys take care," he told them.

He turned to Danny and the attack team and grabbed their necks pulling their heads together.

"I love you guys. We are depending on you but be careful. Remember we are not kids anymore."

At that moment water arrived at the pipe. The back pressure hardened the hose. It made a cracking popping sound as it hit some of the kinks and bends in the line. Like a giant boa constrictor the hose bucked and jumped then settled into a poised position ready to be moved into the fire. The shinny brass Larkin pipe was ready to vomit volumes of water on the fire. Danny stood and opened the nozzle a crack. The compressed air sounded like a freight train releasing steam with a long hiss. The Larkin pipe coughed and spit then produced water in a powerful stream. Danny said, "Come on guys let's kill this son of a bitch." They took their first step back into fire combat.

Molly Means was really scared now. The windows of the intensive care unit were tempered glass. They were sealed shut for hygienic control. That meant she could not open them to be rescued by ladder. She had no idea how fast the fire was moving. She had not an inkling how long they would be safe in this location. The room was filling with smoke and getting warmer. To make matters worse her cell phone had stopped working and some of the kids were crying. Heavy smoke was rolling by the windows. Molly was having difficulty seeing what was going on outside. After the explosion the lights had gone out. Apparently the blast destroyed the utility generators used as emergency power backup. It was a hairy situation. Molly knew she could not panic. Their lives depended on it.

Molly picked up Lulu and held her close. She kissed her tender cheek and whispered softly to the child. Babies understand reassuring tones and body language even if they don't understand words. "I wish you were mine," Molly cooed.

"Come on kids, let's sit in a circle and hold hands." she said.

There was less smoke near the floor and Molly thought that staying low was a good idea. She said a silent prayer that rescuers would find them quickly. She double checked to make sure each child had shoes on. If things got worse they may have to move to find a way out.

Molly's mind was racing a mile a minute. This was a good news bad news situation. The bad news was the probability they were not going to survive this fire. The good news was she had traded shifts with Julia Keats. Julia was the oldest nurse on the staff. Or was it bad news? No, it was good news because Julia was in terrible shape physically. She was close to retirement. Molly was sure that Julia would not be able to handle this situation. Molly was thirty years old and kept herself in good shape. She jogged every day before coming to work. She was up to the task if she could come up with an escape plan.

Molly decided to check out the hallway. It was the only way out. The fire at the back of the building was slowly working its way forward. She told the kids to stay put and eased the door open. She peered into a scene of devastation. The explosion had created a crack that ran the length of the corridor. Both sides of the hall were leaning in. It looked like the floor had snapped like a match stick from the force of the blast. There were open areas where Molly could see bright yellow flames burning on the floor below. She had to get to the stairwell to see if they could escape that way.

She winced from the gash in her leg as she moved out into the hallway. There was smoldering black smoke filling the upper part of the passageway. She crawled on her hands and knees holding onto the wall railing. At best it was going to be difficult to move the children through this area. Molly had to keep one hand on the support rail at all times. A few times she slipped and slid toward the opening in the floor. She clenched her teeth and crawled the last few feet to the stairwell door. Turning the knob she tried to open the door. Was it locked? No, it was jammed shut by the collapse of the building. Molly realized that staying in the IC unit was their only option. Molly hurried back to the room. The cut on her leg was still bleeding and she was getting light headed from smoke inhalation. Molly got back into the room and sealed the door. She pulled the children close and comforted them to keep them calm. Survival now depended on how fast firefighters could find them.

Chapter Seven

Officer Kelley and his partner were in deep trouble. They were caught in a double trap. The building collapse wedged them into a space approximately six feet wide by four feet high by fifteen feet long. Mel Dupree was embedded in waist deep debris. His left foot was hanging through a hole in the floor and was slowly being crushed by the building as it settled after the explosion. It was completely dark and the confined space started to fill with smoke. They were both digging with broken boards to free Mel.

Kelly reached for his prep radio. It was missing from its holster on his belt. "Damn it Mel my radio is gone."

"You better find it asshole or when I get out of this hole I am going to beat you with this board." Mel shouted.

They were drenched in sweat and covered with dust and chunks of debris. Mel was digging on both sides of his body like a man paddling a canoe. Kelly started to look for the radio. Without communications it would be difficult for rescuers to find them. Kelly heard a muffled page and the voice of the dispatcher calling him. He couldn't understand the words but the sound came from the far end of the tomb they were trapped in. He quickly scuttled to the end of the enclosure and flashed his light into the corner. He was confronted by a mixture of fallen beams, pipes, and wires. He could barely make out the winking light on the radio.

Apparently he had dropped it when he moved to help Mel. It was out of his reach. The fallen beams prevented him from getting close enough to grab it.

Kelly broke off a piece of wire that was hanging from the ceiling. He fashioned a retrieving tool with a hook on the end. He reached as far as he could under the fallen beams. There was a metal ring on the side of the radio. If he could get the wire hook into it he would be able to retrieve his radio. Suddenly there was a sharp crack and the beam above his arm dropped. Kelly was pinned in a prone position. It hurt like hell

"I got a problem. A damn beam fell on me," Kelly said to his partner.

"We both got a problem. Can you get the radio?" Mel asked.

"No but I should be able to free this arm with a little digging."

"Hurry up, Kelly, I need help. What ever has my leg is starting to tighten up."

Officer Kelly started to laugh out loud. Mel screamed, "What the fuck are you doing back there reading a joke book?"

"No, my arm is stuck and I am thinking this 'Perils of Pauline' bullshit is starting to get ridiculous. I'm scared out of my wits and everything we do makes things worse. I can see the radio, I can hear the radio, but I can't reach the radio. Now I'm trapped under this damn beam."

"Well I'm scared too and your idiot laughing is not helping the situation."

Mel was making progress. He had removed most of the broken plaster and debris from around his legs. His trapped foot was still hanging through the hole in the floor. If he could manage to twist it around he might be able to get free. He had to hurry because the building was still in motion. The explosion had caused stresses and strains. The supporting structures were still giving way to unaccustomed loads. There was a lot of pressure on his foot. If he didn't get free soon it would be crushed. He found a two by four and drove it down next to his leg. He managed to get it into the hole next to his foot. It took a lot of strength but he was able to position the board so it would act as a wedge to keep the crack in the floor open. He realized this was only a stop gap measure. They needed help before the wedge and his foot were crushed.

When Danny and his crew stepped into the building they knew they couldn't put the fire out. The best they could hope for was to stop it from advancing further. With luck they might even be able to roll it back in some areas. Danny knew they were going to take a beating just standing their ground. Their holding action was critical in allowing the rescue team enough time to find the trapped victims and get them out.

The heat was intense but tolerable for experienced firefighters. Danny and his team dropped to their knees as they began to advance the line toward the rear of the hospital. The Larkin pipe was giving them a good strong stream of water. As the water cut through the smoke looking for flames it started to knock things around. The pressurized flow of water had the power to turn over tables and move chairs. The advancing firefighters could hear the breaking glass. Objects were hurled violently around the hallway as the water stream hit them. All this chaos created more danger for the firefighters. They had to be careful not to cut themselves on broken glass as they crawled forward. The disarray in their path would be a challenge.

Advancing a two and a half inch line is a difficult task. The hose is heavy once it is filled with water and it takes muscle to drag it forward. It is easy to understand why man power is so critical at the scene of a fire. When a line is snaked into an area it becomes looped and coiled as firefighters find their way to the seat of a fire. This adds danger to the situation. The hose is used to extinguish the fire but it is also a life line to get out of a fire. Because there is no visibility in a smoke filled environment it is sometimes necessary to follow the hose by touching it with your hands. When a firefighter comes to a loop or stack of coils it is easy to become confused and go the wrong way. This can be a fatal mistake when trying to get out in a hurry. These things were on Danny's mind as he took his crew deep into the fire involved building.

I was at the fire with Danny where we lost Tommy Jones. The fire was in the basement of a department store. We were with the attack team. Tommy Jones was on the pipe. Danny and I were backing him up. We had moved in a long way and twisted and turned around obstacles as we moved. We were disorientated but knew we could follow the hose out in an emergency.

The fire took a turn for the worse. It grew hotter and the smoke thickened. We were losing the battle. We could hear Chief 7 yelling for us to get out. My heart was beating so hard I thought it would jump out of my body.

"We got to get out of here," Danny shouted.

"You guys take off. I'll hold the fire a few seconds while you get out. I will be right behind you," Tommy yelled.

We gave him a pat on the back and took off following the line with our hands. We paused at the bends and coils to be sure we were going the right way. We found the stairs and scrambled to safety. We waited for Tommy. He never came out. When we found his body it was headed the wrong way next to the hose only a few feet from several coils in the line. That vivid image was in Danny's mind as he moved farther into the smoke and flames of this fire.

The attack procedure for manning a hose line is to have one man handling the pipe. Close behind him will be one or more men dragging the line as the crew moves forward. The second and third man on the line will be leaning in to the pipe man's back giving him support. The pipe man will take the brunt of the heat from the fire. In a prolonged attack the team will change positions to give the point man a break.

By now Danny and the guys had moved about thirty feet into the building. The heat was intense and the smoke thickened with each step forward. They were winded and feeling the effects of the battle. Barkley was soaked in sweat. His muscles ached and he had a raging headache from the booze he drank at the wedding. He was sucking air so hard he could feel the mask collapsing on his face. He yelled for Danny to stop.

"I thought you would never ask," Danny gasped.

They were taking a beating and no one wanted to be the first to admit it. Mac Pierce wasn't saying much. He was third on the line behind Danny and Barkley. They collapsed to the floor. Danny was sitting holding the nozzle with both hands. He was directing water deep into the foreboding smoke trying to halt the advance of the fire. Barkley sat back to back with Danny. Mac Pierce was on his belly directly behind his team mates.

Their efforts so far had exhausted the men. Mac was not faring well. He was sweating at a prodigious rate and becoming dehydrated. He was starting to get heart palpitations which is a sign of potassium loss in the blood stream. He needed to slow down if he was going to last until the job was done. Mac was also gasping for air. He knew the accelerated pace of breathing would quickly deplete his air supply. Mac Pierce had not worked this hard in years and they had only been in this fire for five minutes.

Danny sensed his crew was running out of gas. What the hell could you expect from a bunch of guys over sixty years old?

Danny said, "We are going to make a stand here for a few minutes. Mac, you go outside and cool down. Bring some extra air bottles when you come back. We are going to run out of air shortly and can't leave to get a fresh supply. We will have to change are tanks right here."

Mac turned and headed for the entrance. He knew Danny was right about the air bottles and he really needed to cool down.

The open doorway was a welcome sight. Mac Pierce stumbled and fell as he came outside. Steam vapors were coming off his fire coat. His helmet made a clattering sound as it fell and hit the driveway. Mac pulled off his face piece and sucked in the sweet northern Michigan air. He was on his hands and knees with his head down. He remained in that position until he caught his breath. He rolled over to a sitting position and glanced over at Bobby Kazoo tending the pumper. Bobby started to run toward Mac thinking he was in trouble. Mac waved him off as he struggled to his feet.

Mac looked at the building to see how much the fire had grown. It appeared they were holding the blaze at bay so there was still a decent chance to get to those kids on the fifth floor. Mac knew the interior attack was also supposed to stop the fire from getting to those cops caught somewhere in the collapsed part of the building. The kids were in real trouble if the fire moved past them on the lower floors. If that happened they would be cut off from Joe's rescue team. The only other option was for them to somehow get to the roof or come out the windows. Mac also knew it would take a strong person to break out the windows of the intensive care unit. The glass panes were extra thick. They were hermetically sealed to insure the atmospheric integrity of the room. There was the added problem of finding a ladder long enough to reach the fifth floor. The two rigs on the scene were hose carriers and only carried short ground ladders. Those ladders were not long enough to reach the trapped kids.

On a positive note, Bobby Kazoo had things running smoothly on the outside of the fire. He had the J-model delivering a good supply of water to Danny and the attack team. He began to put the antique Arhens Fox into service. He yelled to the people watching the fire for help and started backing the old rig to a position near the burning hospital. When Bobby jumped out of the Arhens Fox he ran to the rear storage compartment and started rummaging through the tools.

Bobby sorted through the conglomeration of extra nozzles, hose connectors, steel chimney balls, and exotic fire fighting tools. He marveled at the way each piece had been polished and cared for. He knew that volunteer department didn't go to a lot of fires. He knew the volunteers spent many hours training and preparing for action. All their equipment was in top shape. He came across several chains wrapped around elongated rods that resembled long tent pegs. He wondered what they were for as he tossed them to the ground. Eventually he found what he was looking for.

He picked up two devices that were called iron men. They were three foot long steel tripods that could be attached to the ground.

He turned to the group of people who gathered to help him and explained what he had in mind, "We are going to secure these things to the ground facing the fire. I want them pointed toward the rear of the building where the most fire is. A couple of you guys start peeling hose off the pumper and get two large nozzles. We are going to set up some heavy water streams and attach them to these iron men. I can deliver more pressure to these lines once they are secured."

Following directions the volunteers drove the spiked feet of the iron men into the ground. They attached the hose and nozzles and tied them securely in place. Bobby got into the cab of the Arhens Fox, revved the engine, and took off for the hydrant next to the working J-model. Both hose beds peeled off line like fishing reels setting out trolling lines. Men were waiting at the hydrant. They attached the soft suction to the previously installed hydrant gate.

The hose butts were detached and hastily hooked up to the pump outlets of the Arhens Fox. Bobby threw open the water control levers and the old rig began to pump water to the fire. The nozzles strained against their iron man shackles and began to throw huge volumes of water into the fire. The crowd roared their approval and Bobby grinned a toothy grin. Mac grinned too as he put on his mask. He grabbed three extra tanks and moved back into the doorway to hell.

Chapter Eight

The unfolding tragedy was being addressed on several fronts. The 911 operator had notified the State Police Post. She reported that all fire units were out of town and could not be expected back for at least an hour. She explained there was a group of retired firefighters responding to the scene. The firefighters were making an attempt to get trapped victims out of the building. Power lines were down and the power company had been alerted. They were en route to the scene. The State Police desk sergeant sent out a call for all off duty personnel to report to the fire. Bobby Kazoo organized men from the crowd to help out. They set up the two iron men nozzles that were now holding the fire at bay on the upper floors of the building. There was a lot of action going on but it remained a perilous situation.

Borza, Lee Long, and Chum Dupree were on the move. They entered the building through the front door. Their plan was to follow the same path the trapped officers had taken. The scene they found was chaotic. The explosion and collapse had blown debris and dust down the first floor hallway. Fleeing occupants had knocked over furniture and the area was askew with broken glass and bits of clothing. It was a familiar scene for Borza and Long. Their years of responding to disasters prepared them for the chaos. Water was ankle deep on the floor. This was a good sign. It meant someone was managing to get water to the fire.

Borza said, "Let's go guys."

They put on there mask face pieces and started forward to begin the search. They flashed their lights on the first floor hallway doors. The doors were jammed shut. Lee Long drove his Halligan bar into the crack between the double doors and leaned back pulling with all his strength. He pulled so hard his feet began to slip. Chum jumped in to help and slowly they started to pry the doors open. With a loud splintering sound the doors gave way. The header above the doors groaned and settled another inch or two. A mixture of dust and water fell on them.

They were in a crouching position as they squeezed through the opening. They moved their flash lights over the area looking for victims. What they saw was appalling. The weight of the collapsing building had pancaked down leaving the hallway a mass of crushed boards and plaster. Anyone still in there was dead.

Borza discovered a small opening above their heads. One by one they moved through it. They intended to get above the collapsed floor and move down the second floor corridor.

Borza told Chum, "Stay here until I call for you. We may get disorientated in this mess and need a way out. We will stay in voice contact with you. You will be our link to safety. Contact the dispatcher to give an update and see if you can call your buddies on the radio."

Chum activated his radio. "This is officer Chum Dupree reporting I am with a three man rescue crew. We have entered the building to conduct a search. Do you have any further contact with the trapped officers?"

"No. The last report said they were inside looking for people. No further contact. I get no response to my calls. My radio monitoring indicator shows their radio is still on and operating."

Chum sat perched on a pile of debris next to the hole the firefighters had just crawled into. He could feel the sweat running down his body from his arm pits. His uniform was soiled and torn. He was not accustomed to the breathing apparatus he was wearing. He was uncomfortable and apprehensive. He could still see the two old firefighters as they crawled away from him on their hands and knees. They looked like a couple of lumbering grizzly bears as they slowly moved forward. They were leaving a trail of boards and junk as they moved obstacles in their way. Inch deep water was flowing down the destroyed passage way. It resembled a shallow rippling brook as it bubbled between and around them. Chum noticed something floating in the water. He grabbed it as it was about to cascade down the small water fall at the end of the passage way where he sat. It was a prep radio with a blinking light.

Chum yelled to Borza and Long., "They must be up there somewhere. I got their prep radio. It floated down that river you guys are kneeling in."

The rescuers knew they were in an extremely dangerous situation. The building was highly unstable. The way the header above the entry way had dropped a few inches was proof the building was still settling. The super structure was being eroded as the fire progressed. The heavy volume of water, being thrown onto the fire, didn't help the stability of the structure. Water weighs about eight pounds per gallon. A fire engine can deliver over 1000 gallons per minute so the added weight of the water increased the chance of a sudden collapse.

Working in confined spaces is a high risk business. It's like exploring a cave with a wild animal lurking somewhere ahead of you. It's exhausting work and cannot be done if you are claustrophobic. Wearing full turnout gear and having a Scott air pac on your back makes it doubly exhausting. There are a lot of problems but the most aggravating is having your air tank catch on something as you move forward. The job of a tunnel rat is tough. It is not a task for the faint hearted.

Borza and Long were experienced tunnel rats. They had worked at numerous disasters in their thirty years on the job. The big trick is to not get trapped yourself. This takes caution and patience. It is hard to keep your composure when victims are screaming and yelling for help. Holding the hand of a dying person is sometimes part of the job.

I recalled being on a run to the Delray Edison plant in Southwest Detroit. I was riding Squad 4 that night. My running mates were Borza and Long. Central dispatch was sending a full box alarm to a trapped man situation. We knew it was going to be a job that required manpower. When we arrived the guard told us a worker had fallen into a vat of pelletized coal. He directed us to the top floor of the furnace building. The Edison facility was huge. The power station supplied electrical service to a portion of Detroit and many downriver communities. The building was eight stories high and covered two acres. It was an old plant that used coal to generate energy. It was constructed of brick and steel. There were six enormous smoke stacks that produced ugly black smoke. In 1920, when it was built, it was the jewel of the Edison Company. It was now an outdated facility.

When we entered we were deafened by the noise. We had to yell to speak to each other. There was a constant roaring sound interspersed by loud hisses and rumbles. It reminded me of the sounds made by a steam locomotive. Laced though all this noise was the steady buzzing sound of high voltage electricity. Giant furnaces surrounded by steel grated walkways were adding an oppressive heat to the building. It looked like a depressing place to work.

We were directed to a steel staircase that extended up to the fifth floor. We had been sleeping in our dormitory less than five minutes ago. Our bodies were still waking up as we faced the strenuous task of climbing five floors carrying all our gear and tools.

Lee Long complained, "Damn it, why does everyone have to be trapped on the fifth floor?"

"Yeah and why do I always get stuck with carrying these Jaws of Life? They must weigh 50 pounds or more," Borza grumbled.

We were all bitching as we struggled up the stairs. We knew this was the easy part. The real work was waiting for us on the fifth floor.

When we got to the top we found an amazing situation. There were several workers standing around looking down into a huge circular structure that resembled a large swimming pool. It was the top of a big hopper or silo that fed pelletized coal to the furnaces. It measured thirty feet across and was at least thirty feet deep. A thundering metallic banging noise was coming from the bowels of the device. We stepped to the edge and peered down.

We saw a man buried up to his waist in the coal. He had his hands in front of his body and appeared to be holding on to something that had disappeared beneath the coal. When we finally focused on what he was holding the hairs went up on the back of my neck. He was holding a man's face. The rest of the body had vanished below the coal. We had to act quickly.

"What the hell is that thundering roar?" Borza wanted to know.

One of the workers explained it was the feeder hopper for one of the furnaces. The process involved filling the container with 50 or 60 tons of pelletized coal. A four by four door is opened at the bottom of the hopper and the coals start falling on a moving conveyer belt. The conveyer leads to the pulverizing room. We learned that the pulverizing room contained steel balls that resembled large bowling balls. The room was shaped like a section of a rocket booster. The apparatus would spin rapidly and the flying steel balls would turn everything that came into the room to dust. The coal dust was then blown into the furnace for complete efficient burning. The two men at the bottom of the pit were headed for the pulverizing room if we could not save them.

Borza and Long gave me the ropes they were carrying and I fashioned a knotted set up we call a rescue rig. Upon finishing they slipped them on like parachute harnesses. The main knot in this set up is positioned at your chest. When a person is lowered or pulled up he can hold on to the rope and the knot will not tighten to crush him.

Our Captain was giving orders. He said, "No one goes into that pit until we get the machine turned off. Who knows how to shut this thing down?"

"Can't you just go down there and pull them out?" The Forman asked.

The Captain wheeled and glared at the Forman. "Where's the god damn shut off switch?"

"Right here on this panel," volunteered one of the workers.

"Wait. You may destroy a million dollar machine. The hopper must be empty when shut down," the Forman yelled as the Captain headed for the control panel.

"We'll just have to take that chance, won't we," the Captain replied as he slammed the switch to the off position.

There was an oppressive mugginess in the room as the awful vibration and humming noise subsided. The pulverizing machine slowed and came to a halt. You could still hear the thuds and bangs of the steel balls as they rolled to a stop at the bottom of the pulverizing chamber.

"OK guys, let's get in there and tie those workers off," the Captain ordered.

It was a scary place to be. Borza and Long displayed courage by going into that pit. The pelletized coal was still loose. It had the characteristics of quick sand and was slowly sucking the trapped workers under. In fact the face we had seen being held by one of the workers had disappeared beneath the coal. We had to move fast.

Borza and Long scuttled and swam across the coal to get to the buried workers. Their safety ropes extended from their harnesses and were tied off at the top of the hopper.

"We're here to get you out pal," Borza told the man buried up to his waist.

The man's eyes were glazed with fear as he pleaded, "Please hurry. I can't hold on to Willie much longer."

Long reached down and frantically dug with his hands. He uncovered Willie's face again. Willie spit out black mucus as he cleared his mouth of the dirt he swallowed.

"Lord please get me out of here," he begged.

Borza secured a line around the first man while Lee Long cleared enough coal to uncover Willie's whole head.

Neither of the victims could be freed for over a half hour. The problem was the suction of the pelletized coal. It created a bond that acted like glue. It was difficult to break loose. Willie was uncovered to his knees before we could pull him free. The workers expressed their gratitude as soon as we pulled them out of the vat. The first victim was shaking everyone's hand and Willie was hugging and kissing Borza. We walked away from that incident with a good feeling. The suction power of that wet pelletized coal was incredible. We learned something that night.

The situation for the trapped police officers was growing desperate. When Officer Kelly described their predicament as a "Perils of Pauline" scenario he was understating matters. The explosion and collapse of the building had entombed them. The fire was relentlessly moving toward them. They were in complete darkness and had lost their radio. Mel managed to dig himself out of the debris but his foot was still firmly wedged in the crack in the floor. The building was still settling and Mel's foot was in danger of being severed. They were surrounded by devastation and breathing was becoming more difficult. Kelly managed to free his arm and huddled near his partner.

A new danger entered their enclosure. The water that was running through the collapsed hallway was beginning to fill the room. It was like being in a bath tub with a clogged drain.

"Can you believe this shit," Kelly said. "We might drown in this fricken fire. Ain't that a scream?"

"Quit the bullshit and give me a hand with this wedge. We have to let the water out of this area." Mel replied.

The water was already a foot deep. The entire distance from the ceiling to the floor was only four feet so they had to act quickly. They started to seesaw the wedged two by four back and forth. Slowly they were able to extract it. When it came out there was a sucking sound as the warm water started to drain. The respite lasted only moments before the downward moving debris again clogged the hole. Kelly cursed and plunged the two by four up and down with a renewed vigor. They had to keep the drain hole open. It was a terrible situation.

Borza and Long were making progress. They were out of Chum's sight. Their movement had taken them through a few twists and turns. The water flowing around them was warm. This told them the water had passed through the fire before it became run off. They were in single file crawling on their knees most of the time. Every now and then they would yell back to Chum Dupree to keep contact with their escape route. Borza was leading and Long was close behind him. Long kept putting his hand out to touch his partner. He didn't want to lose his buddy in the dark.

Borza grumbled, "Hey jerk off are you enjoying feeling my ass?"

"Yep. It reminds me of Chicago Lil's ass. Remember that old hooker down in the Seventh Battalion who used to come in Kovach's bar and lift her dress to show her pussy for drinks?" Long answered.

Borza laughed out loud as he remembered the old street woman who wore too much makeup and drank enormous amounts of beer. She always came in on payday when the firefighters were raising hell.

"If you remember it right, the guys used to buy her drinks to not show her pussy. It was a horrible sight with that scraggly gray hair and the big brown wart on it."

Long started to laugh too.

There was a crashing sound and Borza was gone. Long knew the area they were crawling on was an accumulation of the shattered materials from the upper floor. Long inched forward and found a hole that led back to the first floor hallway. He peered down and flashed his light on Borza. He was in a sitting position on the floor trying to catch his breath. The fall had knocked the wind out of him.

Between gasps he told Long, We're back on the first floor. I think we can work our way up to the doorway where we left Danny's crew. Get that cop to follow you down and we will complete the search of the first floor. I'm starting to get beat up and it is pissing me off."

Long called Chum forward and helped him through the hole. They were soon hard at work searching for survivors.

A rush of water swirled around them. The water got a few inches deeper than suddenly subsided. 'What the hell was that?" Borza shouted through his mask.

"I don't know. It felt like someone just flushed a toilet," Long answered.

There was no way they could know that Mel Dupree was jamming his wedge up and down the crack in the ceiling to let water out. Mel was in danger of drowning if he couldn't keep the drain unplugged. The Community Hospital was full of life and death drama tonight and the retired firefighters had a part in the play.

Chapter Nine

I was with the team going up for the kids trapped on the fifth floor. This was going to be a scary operation. Climbing five stories in full turnout gear is a formable task. Doing it in a fire involved building is a strenuous undertaking. Doing it when you are over 60 years old is close to impossible.

We huddled with Joe Barchilli as he explained our plan of attack. We were standing at the base of the stairwell near the front of the building.

"I want you to listen carefully," Joe said, "This place is a death trap. If any of you guys get winded or feel you have to stop, let me know. We have to stick together to pull this off. We can only go as fast as the slowest guy. Billy I want your nose right up Bolden's ass. Bob Haig and I will take the lead. Billy I want you to carry three extra tanks. We are going to set up a supply base half way up. OK, let's get going."

There were three coordinated actions now occurring at the scene. Our team was starting a rescue effort to recover the kids on the fifth floor. Borza and his unit were well into the building looking for the missing cops. Danny and his guys were attacking the fire to buy us time. It was going to take a lot of work to pull this thing off.

We were carrying tools and one extra tank each. We started up the stairwell. One of the side walls had fallen outward and the stairway was covered in mounds of shattered plaster. We made the second floor landing and came to a stop. The floor at the turn of the stairwell was gone. Joe flashed his light around and we could see the stairs extending up to the third floor. There was a six foot void separating us from those stairs.

Joe said, "Billy I know you can jump that far but I am not sure the rest of us can. Give it a shot."

The smoke in this area was not too heavy yet. We pulled off our tanks and made room for the kid. Like a big grass hopper he took two steps and easily cleared the chasm. He turned to face us with a smile on his face. We started throwing him our tools, ropes, and tanks. We were huffing and puffing and drenched in sweat.

At this point Joe made a decision, "OK guys let's get rid of this god damn turn out gear. Keep your helmets and boots."

Off came the heavy coats and bunker pants. Shedding twenty pounds of protective gear gave us renewed energy. It was a trade off that was risky but necessary. Fire gear acts like a tough second skin. Without coats and bunker pants we were susceptible to cuts, burns, and bruises. We now felt light and mobile. Joe knew we had to conserve our energy. He ordered us to drop our extra tanks. This would be the site of our supply base.

"Remember this spot Billy. We will be sending you back for these extra tanks."

We still had to get across that six foot opening. Billy was waiting as I made the leap. I hit hard but safe on the other side. Billy caught me as I stumbled forward. I was gasping for air from the effort. I turned to help the others across. Carl Bolden took two steps and landed gracefully on our side of the chasm. It was Joe's turn. He had a bad hip that hindered his jump. He slammed into the edge of the opening and started to slip down. We made a lunge for Joe. Billy was on his belly hanging over the side. He had a firm grip on the seat of Joe's pants. I had one arm and Bolden had his head. We slowly dragged him up to safety.

"You OK Joe?" I asked.

" Yeah but I'm winded. This damn hip is slowing me down"

Billy asked, "Do you want me to lead the way?"

"That might be a good idea Joe. He is stronger and faster. It looks like we may have to move a lot of junk as we move forward," I suggested.

Joe motioned for Billy to move to the front. The kid squeezed by and peered into the darkness ahead. Joe tied a rope around Billy's waist and told him not to go too fast.

We were well aware of the dangers of crawling around in a fire. A fire is like a wild animal when feeding on fuel. It creates its own environment as it burns. Gases and fumes are produced as the fire grows. The fire can devour its own gases and spreads in explosive movements. This is called a flashover. Conditions were ideal for this kind of reaction. There was the added danger of not knowing where the fire was going. In general a fire moves upward but this isn't a hard fast rule. Firefighters do not move past a fire if they can avoid doing so. There is a good chance the fire will seal off escape routes if you make this mistake. Each of us had been trapped at one time or another during our careers. It is not a good feeling. We were facing multiple dangers. There was the chance the building would collapse, the smothering effects of smoke, chance encounters with toxins or burning chemicals, and the possibility of falling through weakened floors. Billy was unaware of these dangers as he led the way upward.

He urged us on, "Come on, my sister is up there some-where and we have to get her out."

Billy was scared but he had a lot of grit. Being with these old men gave him confidence. He felt like he was moving with an entourage of coaches. He relied on our knowledge and direction. His youth made him fearless. He was not sure how he was going to find Lulu but he knew being with these guys was the best way to do it. Billy had seen movies of fires. He was amazed how different the real thing was.

There was an eerie silence punctuated by the crackle of the fire and a distant screeching roar at the rear of the hospital as we started forward again. It was like crawling into a huge spider hole with a tarantula waiting somewhere ahead to pounce on you. The slowly descending smoke and darkness covered us as we moved forward. We could hear the water crashing into the building from somewhere outside.

Billy could hear the raspy breathing sounds of the men's masks behind him. The heat was oppressive. These strange things made Billy's heart beat a little faster. He had that tickle in his stomach that he always had before the kick off of his football games. Finding Lulu was not going to be easy but he was determined to do it.

Billy had been an only child until Lulu arrived. Lulu was a surprise for everyone, especially Billy's mom. At first Billy resented the attention his little sister was getting. She was named Luella Svenson. That name quickly changed to Lulu when the little tyke started cooing and goo gooing in her crib. Billy fell in love with his little sister. The feeling was mutual. When Lulu was upset or frightened she always stretched her arms out for Billy. The bond was strong. Billy was his little sister's protector. Billy knew he had to get his sister out of the danger she now faced. Even if he died trying.

We passed the third floor on the way up. Peering through the glass of the closed door we saw a smoke filled corridor. The fire had not yet extended to this hallway. As we stumbled up the stairs to the fourth floor we knew the situation was changing for the worst. We could feel the temperature change and the smoke got a lot thicker at this level. The closed doors protecting the stairwell on the fourth floor had small fireproof windows. The kind with wire mesh embedded in the glass. The fire rating on these windows was 30 minutes. This meant the glass could sustain a half hour of exposure to a fire before it would shatter and let the flames extend to the next room.

Looking into the fourth floor corridor we were horrified to see the fire boiling angrily as it tried to eat its way to fresh oxygen. The fourth floor was totally involved in flames. The urgency of getting onto the fifth floor to make the rescue was now critical. We knew we were in a race with time. The moment we got above the fire we risked not being able to get out using the stairwell. We were stepping into a trap. There were no other options.

Joe tugged Billy's belt as he led us up the stairs. He told Billy to go back and bring up as many air bottles as he could carry. Billy turned and moved past us on his way down to get the spare tanks. The rest of us collapsed in a heap of old bones and sore muscles. I ached all over. I knew my comrades were hurting too. Things had moved quickly over the last twenty minutes. We had gone from having a good time at the wedding to the brink of disaster.

Joe patted my shoulder and asked, "How you doing trooper?"

"My ass is dragging and my heart is beating so fast it scares me," I answered.

Bolden shook his head and said, "Will you guys quit bitching. You were born for this kind of thing."

"You're right Bolden, I kind of enjoyed it thirty years ago but it isn't fun anymore. It's god damn hard work," I answered.

We could hear Billy wrestling with the spare air bottles as he made his way up the stairs. They were making a metallic clanking sound with every step he took. We were about to embark on the last leg of our rescue attempt. We were not sure the kids were still alive but we had to find them anyway. Kids are resilient. If they were overcome by smoke there was a chance we could resuscitate them. We were determined to find them.

"Everyone put on a fresh air tank," Joe ordered.

Changing air bottles in a smoke filled environment can be tricky. The tank on your back has to be disconnected and the new bottle installed swiftly. Your time frame to do this is as long as you can hold your breath. Any foul ups in the procedure and you will have to share a partners mask and buddy breathe from his tank. It is a lot like scuba divers under water when one member runs out of air. Joe supervised the changing of the tanks. It was done quickly and professionally. We were ready to find those kids. We were on our last tank. We had thirty minutes of air left. We started to move. This time Joe took the lead. We needed all his expertise to get us through this harrowing rescue attempt.

Joe was dead tired. He knew the movement down the last hall was going to be brutal. He was glad he had included the kid in the rescue team.

Joe gave final instructions, "I want you guys to keep pushing as hard as you can. The fire is growing in intensity. If the kids are still sealed in the IC room with the nurse they are temporarily safe. The trip down the corridor is going to be a bitch. If for some reason I can't make it, I want you to leave me and get into that room. Do you understand?"

I shouted, "Bullshit Joe. We are not going to leave anyone. We never did when we were on the job and we are not going to do it now."

Joe reached out and grabbed the front of my shirt. He leveled a stare that would have stopped a charging bull in its tracks.

"Bob you have know me for a long time. Frankly I don't know how I made it this far. Don't give me a hard time on this. We both know what is involved here. I have survived a lot of fires and I will make it out of this one too."

I lowered my eyes and said, "You're right Joe. Let's get moving before it is too late."

Joe turned and led us toward the smoldering hallway.

Chapter Ten

The crew trying to hold the fire back was losing ground. The flames were making a frontal assault on the men crouched in the hallway. With octopus like arms the fire was probing and reaching to encircle the firefighters. The fire was seeking oxygen. The flames snaked up the walls and along the ceiling in a cloak of dirty hot smoke. Any hole or crack would do. Once the fire entered a new area it would flash and flare invigorated by the fresh air. Like a tsunami wave it consumed all in its path.

Danny was on the pipe. He was leaning into the back pressure of the hose. He was breathing hard. His mask was demanding air at more than the normal rate. Barkley and Pierce were right behind him. Visibility was at zero and he was taking a beating from the heat.

Barkley shook Danny's shoulder and shouted, "Take a break partner. Let me have the pipe." Danny shook his head and moved to the second position on the line.

"It's getting damn hot in here. Maybe we should move back a little," Pierce said.

"We can't until we know how the rescue team is doing. We have to give them as much time as possible," answered Danny.

Firefighting is a team activity. A ladder crew will hustle to open up a building when men are advancing a hose line so the nozzle men will not be caught in a backdraft. A coordinated attack will have men on the roof chopping holes so the fire will move toward fresh air. The pipe men will be inside ready to apply water the moment they see the flames flare up in the smoke. Everyone involved in attacking a fire is at risk. They have to depend on each other.

Danny and his team were going to hold their ground. They would stay put until they were sure the rescue units got everyone out of the building. Little did they know how difficult the rescues were going to be.

The cops, Jim Kelly and Mel Dupree, were desperate. They had the sinking feeling they were caught in a large coffin. There was no visibility and the smoke mingled with plaster dust was getting thicker. Their real concern was the water now rushing through the area they were trapped in. It was starting to fill the room. Mel was especially worried because his foot was still caught in the crack in the floor.

In the darkness Mel felt something scramble up his arm and over his head.

"Holy crap I think a rat just ran over me," he yelled.

There was the sound of several scurrying creatures and a numerous frightened squeaks.

"Whoa, damn it there's something in here with us," Kelly answered.

Both men were terrified and started to flail and swing at the unseen creatures. It didn't take long to realize the rats who occupied the building were trying to escape just like the humans were. The rats were swept away when thousands of gallons of water had been hurtled into the building by the big lines working outside. The water carried the rats through the cracks and crevices of the collapsed walls into the same enclosure with the trapped men. The rodents darted from one end of the tomb to the other seeking an escape route. During their frantic search they scrambled repeatedly over the spooked men. Amidst the scratching and squeaking was the primal cry of Mel as he clutched and threw rats from his body. They did not bite him. They only wanted to get out.

70

There were dozens of panicked rats. The skittering and scratching sound of their movement filled the room. One of them ran down Mel's leg and found the opening next to the wedge in the cracked floor. The rest followed. Mel screamed and thrashed as they moved down his body. In moments they were gone. The room became silent again. The silence was punctuated only by the heavy breathing of the men as they tried to regain their composure.

Meanwhile Molly Means was going through her own ordeal. Smoke was slowly penetrating the sealed openings of the intensive care unit. The children were getting uncomfortable and started to whimper and cry. Molly prayed that someone would rescue them She had taken every the towel and sheet she could find and soaked them in water. She packed them into every opening that was seeping smoke. It was a losing battle. The relentless smoke was still coming in. She sat mesmerized as the smoke curled and coiled trying to fill the room. Like a cobra bobbing and weaving when it rises from a fakir's basket the smoke slowly moved toward the ceiling. Molly figured it was only a matter of time before the intruding smoke would subject them to a choking smothering death.

She glanced quickly around the room for help. Maybe the oxygen tanks can buy us some time she reasoned. Gathering every tank she could find she stacked them against the wall near the door where she and the kids were huddled. Next she took the plastic canopies off the beds used by the respiratory patients. She fashioned a small tent like enclosure by securing the plastic to the wall with thumb tacks and draping the sheets over two chairs. Using books and toys she secured canopy to the floor. The job was finished by piling wet towels and clothing around the bottom as a smoke barrier. It was crude and flimsy but it was the best she could do.

Her thoughts were to wait until the descending smoke reached the top of the little tent then to open the valve on one of the oxygen bottles. In effect Molly was creating a large positive pressure enclosure that would hold the smoke out like a firefighters self contained breathing apparatus. The principal was the same. The pressure in the tent would temporally be greater than the pressure outside. This would hold back the killing smoke. Molly knew they could only stay in the tent until they used up the oxygen bottles. Would it work? Only time would tell. Molly had no other ideas. They would have to sit tight and wait for the firefighters.

After Borza recovered from falling through the ceiling he gathered his team together again. Long called Chum forward and they dropped through the hole Borza created when he fell. They were still in the first section of the corridor. They made a quick check by looking into the rooms as they moved down the hallway. In the second section they had to enter each room because the smoke was too heavy to see. The sagging second floor created a problem by jamming the room doors so they could not be opened. The glass on these doors had to be broken. Borza and Long climbed in and out of each room making a search. It was brutal work and the men were starting to tire.

Water and chunks of plaster were coming down as the team prepared to force the door to the last section of the corridor. Borza told the men to stand back as he smashed the glass out of the door. With a mighty swing he hit the reinforced window. It shattered and hung on the safety wire woven between the panes. Borza flipped his axe and hooked the pointed peen into the wire and ripped it out.

Something hit him in the chest followed by more squeaking squealing objects. It was the same rats that had terrorized the trapped cops. The rats jumped and ricocheted off Chum and Long. They bounced around and over the men. It was over in a second.

"What the hell was that?" asked Chum.

"I think they were rats," answered Borza. "You guys OK?"

"We're OK. I think we should be following those rats. They got the right idea," Long replied.

When they entered the last section of the hall they found the smoke was hotter and thicker. They knew they were nearing the fire suppression team because they could hear the crash of the water beating back the flames.

"I can hear Danny and the guys up ahead. If the cops are past this area they are lost. Our only hope is to find them somewhere on the upper floors," Lee Long shouted through his face piece.

Chum Dupree was worried about his brother Mel and Officer Kelly. He was also scared out of his wits. He had no idea how much physical effort was involved in firefighting. His strength was being drained from wearing the heavy gear and being in the confining grip of the air mask. Borza and Long were the ones who crawled into the rooms to search for victims. Chum wondered how those old guys could still be standing.

Breaking out the door window sent a rush of oxygen toward the fire. The room lit up. There was a flaring of flames near the ceiling. Danny O'Brien and his crew had to roll on their backs to whip the line around over their heads to beat back the charging fire.

"What the fuck is going on back there?" Danny bellowed.

"It's us looking for the cops. Do you have extra air bottles up there?" Borza answered.

"Yeah, come on up and get them. They're by the door you will see them when you come forward."

The three rescuers crawled through the broken window and started to move ahead in a crouched position because the flaring fire was making the upper part of the corridor hotter.

The trapped officers were on the verge of panic. The tremendous volume of water being hurled into the building was flooding the area in which they were confined. Mel's ankle was caught in the crack and he could barely keep his head above the rising water. The water was running down his leg and out to the floor below but plaster and dust was constantly plugging the hole. Mel had a broken two by four that he kept thrusting up and down next to his leg to keep the water draining. It seemed to be a losing battle.

They needed rescue and they needed it quickly. Suddenly a searing pain hit Mel's foot. It was so intense he started to scream. Kelly rushed to help his partner. "What's wrong Mel? What's going on?"

"My god damn foot is on fire. Help me."

All Kelly could do was hold Mel's hands and yell for help as loud as he could.

It was the flaring fire that slipped by Danny's protecting water curtain. It would send out a long tongue to taste Mel's foot periodically. It was not constant but it was painful when the fire reached that part of the ceiling. The smoke shielded the foot from the view of the firefighters moving through the area. When Danny would turn the pipe to wash the ceiling behind him Mel would get temporary relief. Kelly and Mel continued to yell for help.

As the rescue team moved forward they passed directly under the spot where the two cops were trapped.

"Hold it; I think I hear my brother." Chum said.

"Yeah I hear it too Sounds looks its right above us." Borza responded. "Hey Danny whip that line on the ceiling above us again. We think the cops are on the next floor up." They started to shine their flash lights on the ceiling.

"Will you look at that? It's a god damn foot." Long exclaimed.

"Yeah and it has a cop's shoe on it. It has to be my brother's foot. It's moving and they're yelling so we know they are alive. We have to get them out of there as quick as we can."

Borza reached up and gave the dangling foot a couple of tugs. The yelling stopped momentarily then restarted with a renewed vigor.

Mel grabbed Kelly's arm and said," I think they found us. Someone is jerking on my foot. Keep hollering."

"What kind of tools do we have?" Borza asked.

"Between us we have your axe, my Halligan bar, and Chum's pike pole.

"Chum you find that doorway up ahead and go to the rig and ask Bobby Kazoo for couple of sledge hammers. Ask him to find a partner saw so we can cut through the concrete ceiling. I know it has rebar in it. Let's get moving guys," Borza ordered.

Chum took off like a scared cat. He stumbled and crashed to the floor. He was up cursing and quickly out the door. He dumped his tank and mask near the exit. He sprinted to where Bobby Kazoo was controlling the water flow to the fire.

He told Bobby, "We found Mel and Kelly. We need some sledge hammers and a partner saw. We have to hurry. The fire is getting bigger."

"I got hammers but I will have to scratch to find a saw. Take these sledges and I will look for a saw."

The hammers were heavy and hard to carry. He turned to run back to the building. He realized he was winded and seemed to be moving in slow motion. His body was trying hard to keep the adrenaline flowing but he was rapidly running out of juice. He moved back at a slow trot and knelt to put on his breathing apparatus. Someone in the crowd had changed the bottle and assisted him in donning his tank. He was good for another thirty minutes.

Inside, Mac Pierce and Barkley crawled back to where the rescue team was working. They knew help would be needed breeching the ceiling to make an escape hole for the cops. It was going to be exhausting work. With more guys they could spell each other off. Danny would be left alone to face the fire.

The problem they faced was typical of what firefighters face on a daily basis. There is no instruction book to guide them. There is no one else to call. It is a do or die process that relies on experience, ingenuity, and just plain grit. The biggest problem facing the rescuers was if they had enough energy left to do the job. Wielding an eight pound sledge hammer and pounding above your head is a sure formula for a heart attack. When you add smoky conditions, extreme heat, and hot dripping water you have a devil's brew of trouble.

They found a desk. The men dragged it to the center of the hallway. Climbing on top of the desk they went to work. They had to be careful when they swung the sledge near Mel's foot. They did not want to injure him. Borza asked Chum to pull the plaster down with his pike pole so he could see the area underneath the floor. Chum started working on the ceiling. Pulling a ceiling is a dirty job. They were soon covered with wet messy crap. Chum didn't hesitate he kept working with a fervor. He rapidly cleared an area about six feet in circumference. Borza flashed his light into the hole. He saw there was a concrete floor, as he expected, and there was probably terrazzo above that.

"Get down Chum and let Lee Long take a shot with his sledge," Borza ordered.

Chum was glad to get down. It was hot near the ceiling.

Working with a tank on your back is a tough proposition but there is no other way in a fire situation. Lee brought the sledge around in a swing that came from his ankles. It made a wide arc to gain energy and collided with the concrete. The hammer rebounded almost knocking him off the desk. A chunk the size of a tea cup ricocheted off the wall." This is going to be tough," he yelled.

"Five swings each then take a break," Borza instructed.

Soon the men had a working rotation that allowed for a quick break and recovery time from the grueling task. They were showered by chunks of concrete and dust as they pounded on the ceiling. The noise was loud and echoed in the area where they worked. Within minutes they were able to open a one foot by one foot area just below the terrazzo floor surface.

"Stand clear guys because, when I bust through, the second floor is going to take a piss on us," Borza yelled.

He was right. With a mighty blow the opening was completed. The terrazzo shattered and a ton of water mixed with plaster and debris started to drain through the hole.

"Thank you. Thank you," shouted Mel Dupree.

The water that had risen to his chin started to recede. The tomb they were trapped in was still hot and the smoke was getting thicker. Both men were coughing and gagging. Tears ran down their cheeks and snot hung in long strings from their noses. As water poured from the opening smoke poured in to replace it.

Jim Kelly could see the beams of the flashlights penetrating the hole. He scrambled over and shouted for a tool to be passed up so he could help enlarge the opening from above. An eight pound sledge came through the hole. Kelly grabbed it and began to work on the floor. The opening grew larger as the hammers pounded and destroyed the barrier separating the first and second floors. Eventually there was enough space opened for Kelly to get out.

Chum Dupree called for Kelly to come down.

"Bullshit. I'm staying here till we get your brother out and we have to hurry. Things are getting worse up here by the minute."

"Two of you guys hand your air tanks up to them and scoot out of here and get fresh tanks," Borza commanded.

Long and Chum Dupree took deep breaths and slipped out of their harnesses. They quickly passed their masks up through the hole. Staying low and feeling the wall with their hands they dashed for the doorway. They stumbled free into the cool night air.

Danny was being hard pressed by the fire. He knew he had to hold it back until the cops were freed and removed from the building. There were no ear flaps on the old helmets they had taken from the fire station. Danny sustained burns to his neck and ears. He gave a little more ground but clenched his teeth against the pain and continued to hurl water into the raging fire.

"Hurry up guys. This bastard fire is getting meaner and meaner. I don't know how long I can hold it," Danny yelled.

Outside Bobby Kazoo found a partner saw. It wasn't on either of his two rigs. It was on one of the arriving ambulances. In rural communities like Cheboygan the paramedics often service the inter state highways and use the saws to cut people free from auto accidents. Bobby gave the saw to Lee Long who turned and ran back toward the fire. As

Long moved he pulled on the starting rope. He and Chum had fresh tanks and were ready to go to work. By the time they reached the doorway the saw had snorted a few times then started. It sounded like a hive of angry bees as the noise bounced off the walls when they entered the hallway.

"Hurry up. We ain't got much time," shouted Borza.

Chum and Long jumped up on the desk. There was a shower of sparks and powdered concrete as the saw bit into the ceiling. Long leaned into his work with determination. Chum Dupree was right behind him leaning into his back for support Every now and then a finger of flame would appear above the area where they worked. The fire was aggressively attempting to extend down the hallway. The plan was to start cutting about a half a yard from the dangling foot. Beginning at the crack in the floor they would cut an arc around the foot and connect with the crack again. Hopefully this portion of the ceiling would fall free.

The dynamics of the damaged building, which was settling, caused the saw to bind on the parallel cut. Sweat poured down Lee Long's face. His arms ached from holding the heavy vibrating saw above his head. The noise was horrendous. Sparks mixed with dust, dirty hot water, and smoke covered the workers. Long suddenly felt woozy. His body was reacting to the intense stress it had been subjected to over the last half hour. He collapsed dropping the saw. The trigger was locked in the full power position. It bounced off the desk hitting the wall on the rebound. The rotating blade redirected the saw across the hall. It caught Borza on the arm just above the elbow cutting all the way to the bone. Chum tried to catch Long as he fell. They both tumbled from the desk in a heap landing on top of Borza.

Danny heard the clashing clattering racket behind him and called," What's going on back there? Do you need help?"

Borza answered," Long is down and I'm bleeding like a stuck pig. We need to get Long outside?"

Again that old axiom of the fire service had kicked in. When one thing turns to shit everything turns to shit. A domino effect of unfortunate incidents was starting to undermine the efforts of the rescuers. The task of rescuing two trapped persons had escalated to getting three people out of the building.

Borza was clutching his arm which was squirting blood with every beat of his heart. He reached under his fire coat and pulled off his belt. He wrapped it around his arm and with a jerk tightened the belt as tight as possible. He secured the make shift tourniquet and scrambled over to where Lee Long was lying on the floor.

He shouted, "Help me. We have to get him out of here right now."

Only Pierce and Barkley were left to get the cops free. Barkley felt around on the floor for the saw which had stalled and was now hidden by intense smoke. He found it and pulled the rope handle to restart the motor. It kicked in with a buzzing roar. Holding it with one hand he felt around in the darkness for the desk. Slowly he pulled his aching body up and into position to work on the ceiling. He reached up and found the crevasse where Lee Long had been cutting before he passed out. Inserting the whirling blade he attacked the ceiling with a vengeance. The saw bucked and rebounded against Barkley's grip but he held firm. There was no time to waste. The room was growing hotter. Barkley knew they only had a short time to pull this thing off.

Lee Long was unconscious. Chum Dupree grabbed one of Long's arms and Borza grabbed the other. Borza could only use one hand because of his injury. They were crouched low as they dragged the unconscious body toward the doorway. Getting outside meant life or death for Lee Long. They did not know if he had a heart attack or had fainted from exhaustion. They did not know if they were indeed dragging a dead man. They would find out when they got his body outside.

Bobby Kazoo was in control of the activities on the outside of the fire. His years of experience as a fire engine operator in the Detroit Fire Department had given him a PHD in fire fighting. He could read smoke and he knew fire tactics. He was the link to life for the Firefighters inside the building. He recruited civilians to help him and now had several lines tied down delivering huge volumes of water to the fire. He instructed three teenagers how to assist Firefighters in changing bottles when they needed a fresh tank of air. He took portable generators off both rigs and showed a man how to operate them. The generators contributed a steady hum to a noisy scene. The area surrounding the fire was lit up by spotlights hooked to the generators.

Bobby kept his eyes on the door where his guys were working. He saw Borza first. He could see he was injured because one arm was hanging loosely at his side. Chum Dupree crawled out next. They were pulling something. They were covered in smoke and steam was coming off their backs as the cool air hit their hot fire coats. He realized they were bringing someone out. Bobby shouted for the paramedics, who recently arrived on the scene, to help the men as they came out of the fire. The rescuers pulled Lee Long a few yards from the doorway and collapsed in a heap from exhaustion. Bobby was now in a full run just a few steps ahead of the paramedics. When they got there they pulled the men another ten yards away from the boiling heat and smoke coming from the doorway.

Borza and Chum were in a sitting position. They ripped off their masks. Borza was gasping and gagging trying to suck in fresh air. Chum Dupree was gagging and vomiting on himself. One of the paramedics gave a small oxygen breather to Borza before moving to assist Lee Long.

The paramedic checked Long's vital signs. His heart was still beating and there was a strong pulse. His breath was shallow but it looked like Long was going to make it to the hospital. Two more paramedics arrived with a stretcher. They gently slid Lee Long onto the gurney and snapped it into the up position. Bobby Kazoo ran along side as they moved away from the fire. He was holding Long's dirty hand and he talked to his friend. There was no response until they neared the ambulance. Long's eyes began to flicker as consciousness returned.

"What happened?" Long asked.

"You passed out Lee. The guys got you out and you are on the way to the hospital," Bobby answered.

Long glanced back toward the fire and said, "Bobby they ain't got much time in there. We got one cop free but the other one is still hung up. Danny and the guys are doing a hell of a job but I know they are taking a heck of a beating. Bobby they may have to leave that last cop in there unless we get more help."

"Don't worry about that shit Lee. I know those guys like you do. They will pull this thing off and get out safely."

"Damn it, I hope you're right," Long sighed as he closed his eyes.

Chapter Eleven

The women left the wedding. They could see smoke billowing from the fire at the end of town. They had been through this before when their husbands were active Firefighters It was stressful when the media reported that a Fireman had been injured or killed. The Department was pretty good about contacting loved ones when a man was down but the wait for news was agonizing.

They went to the fire station and sat in the kitchen waiting for news from the fire. Coffee was made and they sat in silence for awhile. They knew their husbands were the only thing that stood between rescue and disaster at the hospital. The men were long past their prime. They possessed the experience to do the job but did they have the physical stamina to pull it off? That was the question that worried the women. It was dangerous to be fighting fires past the age of 60. Tonight there was no alternative.

The women began talking about the good times they shared over the years. They reminisced about the fund raisers, the burn tournament, zoo day, and the gala inauguration parties at the union hall. Firefighters were always doing things to help people. The women were part of the culture surrounding the job and it enriched their lives.

The Police Department set up a monitoring post at the station's watch desk. There was a doorway to the kitchen next to the watch desk. The department radio was operating so all could hear what was happening at the fire. Communication between police radios at the scene and the dispatcher gave a blow by blow account of the fire. A police car and one officer remained at the fire hall.

At the fire one of the arriving ambulances supplied Bobby Kazoo with a department radio. From his post, near the two working rigs, Bobby would give periodic updates to the dispatcher at central communications. The dialogue came through the speakers at the fire hall and brought the drama of the fire scene to those listening. It was similar to the war room of an air craft carrier where the actions of fliers can be heard as they engage in combat.

The women were veterans of the 1967 riot in Detroit. They were young women in 1967 and not yet accustomed to the stresses of being married to a Firefighter. The first three days of that civil insurrection took 43 civilian lives. The city lost one police officer and two Firefighters. It was a horrendous time and it lasted a week before order was restored.

It started around 3am on a steamy Sunday morning. Police were conducting a raid on a blind pig near 12th street. In 1967 the Detroit Police Department consisted of mostly white men. The civil rights movement was in full swing at this time and racial tensions were high.

Tactics used were routine. This meant when the police moved in they came hard and fast. Resistance was dealt with swiftly and sometimes physically. Heads would be broken if the police were challenged. It was a policy of maintaining respect for the police and keeping the criminal element in fear of confrontation. The mixture of a Saturday night of drinking, a hot summer eve, and the resentment built up over the years of racial discrimination and perceived hate, emanating from both blacks and whites, exploded into an escalating confrontation that became a week long riot.

Police on the scene could not control the situation. The anger of the gathering crowd caused the raiding officers to call for help. Someone in the crowd set fire to an abandoned store front. More people gathered. Fire companies arrived on the scene and went to work. Another store was set on fire. Then an opportunist hurled a concrete block through a Jewelry store window and started grabbing all the valuables he could carry. This turned the watching crowd into a participating mob.

Glass could be heard shattering up and down the business district of 12th Street. Soon several buildings were on fire. Looters were having a field day grabbing new clothes, TVs, jewelry, and any valuable goods they could carry. It was a looter's holiday and had nothing to do with civil rights. It had everything to do with opportunity and lawlessness. It wasn't long before the first shots rang out. Unarmed Firefighters were being shot at as they tried to save lives and property. These actions spoke volumes about the changes that were to occur in Detroit. An irreversible direction was set for the city. This direction was fueled by the political ambitions of the Colin Wright administration which took office not long after the riot. When a time for healing was needed the Wright administration chose a path of keeping its political regime in control of city hall. Colin Wright and his cronies were successful. How well things worked out for Detroiters is a matter of opinion.

If you were a member of the ruling elite you became enriched with wealth and power. The other 99 percent of Detroiters were caught in a vicious cycle of crime and poverty. The thousands of small businesses that populated the main thoroughfares, like Grand River and Gratiot, were forced to leave the city. With them went the tax base that supported city services. The 1967 riot gutted a once great city and left smoking ruins. Detroit became the murder capitol of America. The bums and bad guys Mayor Wright coddled started a tradition of trying to burn the town down on Devil's Night every year.

The job of Firefighting became more difficult as the city changed. Apparatus that used to carry five and six men were cut to three and four. People who had no concept of what it took to fight a fire were put in charge. They made decisions that were dangerous to Firefighters and civilians alike. It was all part of the cronyism of the Mayor's political team. Through it all the Detroit Fire Department continued to perform at an incredible level of efficiency. Thanks to the Firefighters Union the Mayor was never able to control the promotional system in the department. When people called we arrived on the scene in less than three minutes to help them. We were there and I can assure you the administration could care less.

A statement by Mayor Collin Wright still rings in my ears. We had responded to a fire next door to Engine Four which had recently been closed by the efficiency experts of the Wright administration. I bounded onto the porch to enter the building to search for victims. People were screaming that a little girl was trapped inside. I popped the window with my axe and started to enter the house. Looking down I found a small six year old girl lying a few feet from the window. She had died of suffocation in the smoke. She was next to a window she did not know how to open. She needed a Firefighter. The station next to her house had been closed for less than a week. As I carried the child to a waiting ambulance a TV newsman asked my opinion. I laid the death directly on the Mayor's door step. If Engine Four had been in service I was positive the little girl would still be alive. The Mayor's reply on the evening news was that people die everyday. I was convinced the Mayor felt no responsibility. His only interest was maintaining his political power base.

The wives sitting in the Fire Hall in northern Michigan had been through it all. They supported their men during those agonizing changes in the city that including the severe manpower cuts. Every time the Mayor cut the work force he ratcheted up the danger to the Firefighters. Yet most of them survived. The wedding tonight was a grand reunion for some of those survivors.

The wives consoled and comforted each other. They talked about the 1967 riot. They remembered sitting with their children worrying about their men. It was a week before they saw their husbands again. Two Firefighters were killed during the riot. These memories added to the tension in the room.

They had attended the Department funeral for the Firefighters who had given their lives defending the city during the riot. It was a grand affair with a host of dignitaries in attendance. The caskets were placed on the hose beds of the pumpers from the Fire Companies the men had worked at. The rigs were immaculate, a mixture of shiny red paint and sparkling chrome. The company members accompanying the caskets were all spit and polish. Their uniforms were adorned with the medals they had earned and they wore white gloves. The rigs left the funeral home and moved through the streets of the city. The procession was extremely long. Dignitaries and Fire Officials from across the nation were there to pay their respects. There were representatives from California, Boston, Montreal, and other departments too numerous to mention. And yes the cops were there too. We share the danger of the streets. We are brothers in blue.

Words were spoken and prayers were said. The faces of the Firefighters were grim and reflected the strain of fighting fires in riot conditions. The widows had their small children gathered around them. Each had two babies and none of these kids were over four years old. They did not know they would never see their daddies again. A command was given and the crack of the honor guard rifles rang out. Over head six fighter jets swooped low. Passing over the cemetery, with a roar, two of the planes peeled off and left the formation. It signified the loss of two running mates to the dangers of their profession.

The uniformed pallbearers reached over and folded the American flags that draped the caskets. With a salute the flags were given to the Chief Officer in command. Turning on his heel the Chief marched directly to each widow. He bent low and delivered the flags. One of the young women had her head bowed and gazed into her lap where she clutched all that remained of her husband. A tear rolled down her cheek and splashed onto the flag. The sight of such sacrifice will follow me to my grave.

On this cool night in northern Michigan a group of ladies sat waiting for their men to fight their last fire. They prayed they would never have to attend a Department funeral again. It was heart rending to think they had to face such uncertainty one more time.

The radio crackled as the dispatcher reported a Firefighter had been injured. Every heart in the room skipped a beat. The injured man was not identified and at that moment the watch desk phone began to ring. The police officer picked up the phone to receive the message. He hung up and turned to the women.

"Which one of you is Mildred Long? They report your husband is injured but doing well. I will take you to the hospital."

Mildred gathered her things and was quickly out the door on the way to the hospital. Before she left, Mary Barchilli jumped up and ran after her.

"Wait for me," she called

In tough times it is important to have a shoulder to lean on. The women stuck to each other through thick and thin. They used the same buddy system their Firefighter husbands used. The remaining women sat somberly with heads bowed. The fire was starting to pile up victims.

The hospital they were taken to was not really a hospital. It was a large clinic used for therapy and minor surgeries. There were people milling around when the women arrived. Many were patients who had been evacuated from the hospital fire. The scene bordered on chaotic with people coming in looking for loved ones.

The clinic administrator was a cool character. He came from the strong farmer stock that populated the area. He was not easily rattled. He managed to keep order in a difficult situation. He met Mildred and Mary at the door. He introduced himself and reassured Mildred that her husband was going to be OK. He took her by the arm and led her to a room at the end of the hall.

Entering the room she saw her husband lying in a bed hooked to monitoring devices. His face broke into a big toothy grin. Mildred knew he was going to be alright. She hurried to his side and he gathered her into his strong hairy arms. His strength and her resolve made for a strong marriage. He nuzzled her hair with his face and whispered in her ear, "I love you baby."

"Love you too you big bum,"

Mary watched with a lump in her throat. She pulled two chairs close to the bed and kissed Lee on the cheek. Their eyes connected and Lee paused to gather his thoughts.

"Mary, I ain't going to bullshit you. This fire is a mean one. Joe and his crew have taken on the toughest job. They are going to the top floor and will be above the fire. He has some of the best Firefighters I know with him. The only thing that will stop them is if they run out if gas like I did. Joe was smart and took a strong teenage kid with them. I know he figured the kid could carry one of them out if they went down. It is a coin flip if they can reach the trapped people in time. If Joe can't do it no one can."

"Thanks Lee for being honest with me."

Mary got up and walked to the window. She did not want Lee or Mildred to see the fear in her eyes. She gazed toward the far end of town where the horizon was aglow from the blaze. Around the glow was the darkness of the night. Mary had a sinking feeling in the pit of her stomach. Tears ran down her cheeks. She had a foreboding premonition that one of the guys would not make it through this one.

Chapter Twelve

The smoke was hot and angry on the fifth floor. Joe and the rest of us made it to the hallway door. We sat for a moment gathering our strength trying to figure out the next move. A fire rescue problem is always complicated. Each move is a calculated risk. Our rescue team didn't want to end up having to be rescued like the cops trapped several floors below. The reason was obvious. There was no one left to get us out. It was a one shot deal. A real do or don't with the don't having a fatal conclusion. Of course what happened to the cops could not be predicted. The explosion of the propane tanks was an unlucky surprise. Most rescues are made by fire personnel who know what to expect in a fire environment. The dangerous part of the job is the unknown factors that can kill you in a heart beat.

We were on their hands and knees with our heads close together. The smoke was so thick we could hardly see each other.

"Still got that rope kid?" Joe asked.

"Yes sir and these three extra tanks."

Joe continued," OK guys, I want everyone tied together at eight to ten foot intervals. Bob Haig you tie the knots. I know you can do it because the last time I risked my life on a rope, you hooked me up."

Carl Bolden snorted, "You're so full of shit Joe. You know I am the best knot tier on the department and you haven't admitted it for thirty years."

"Listen fat ass, Bob is tying the knots. I want you and the kid to go in first. I'm keeping the best knot tier with me in case you don't make it and we have to lower those kids by rope."

I yelled at them, "God damn it you guys. We got our asses on the line here and you're still pulling each others chain.

I heard them both chuckle and realized they were pulling my chain. I loved these men. They knew how to reduce the pressure of a tense situation with a little bullshit humor. We had to be relaxed and alert for the next part of this rescue.

During our discussion I was tying the knots to connect this rescue unit together. Joe knew the explosion had ruptured the floor. He was aware that both sides of the hall slanted down at a forty five degree angle toward a gapping crack that oozed smoke and an occasional wisp of flame. While attaching the safety lines to the men my thoughts drifted back to the incident where I had secured a safety line to Joe.

We had responded to an apartment fire in the Cass Corridor. It was a poverty stricken area of cheap hotels, prostitutes, and dope peddlers. A lot of innocent people were caught in this mix. The hotel where the fire was raging housed an assortment of senior citizens and single mothers on ADC. The building was tall. It was a few stories higher than the reach of any ladder truck on the scene.

We later learned a pimp had murdered one of his girls on the third floor. He tried to cover his crime by pouring five gallons of gasoline into her apartment and tossing a match in as he left the room. The resulting blast had blown him down the stairwell in a ball of flame. When we arrived on the scene, Joe and I grabbed the hose roller and rope and dashed for the doorway. Flames were roaring out of the dead prostitute's third floor window. People were screaming and we kept looking up as we entered the building. Experience taught us that people will jump when trapped by fire. Firefighters have been killed or injured by falling bodies when moving into burning high rises.

The first thing we encountered, in the hallway near the entrance, was a man crawling on his hands and knees. He was naked except for his leather belt and a large gold medallion around his neck. The gold medallion, the chain, and his belt buckle were glowing red hot like a branding iron. His eyes were glazed and he had an unseeing stare as he slowly moved toward the doorway. His body was terribly charred. I knew he would die an agonizing death in the burn unit of Receiving Hospital. He was the arsonist and it was a fitting reward for his crime.

Joe and I knew we had to get above the fire floor to guide people out of the growing conflagration. We were young and strong. Our exuberance would not allow our brains to turn on the danger signal. We were fearless. We knew we would live forever. It is amazing how these attitudes change as you get older.

We knew enough not to go up the front stairway. We ran down the first floor hallway and forced open the locked door to the rear stairwell. A problem in many buildings in high crime areas is the doors are usually chained shut. I didn't want to remember how many times we had found bodies piled up at a chained shut door with signs of claw marks and broken finger nails embedded in the wood. We lucked out this time and only had to force the door lock.

It was only a matter of time before the third floor fire burned through the door and created a chimney to the top floors. We bounded up the stairs and went to the roof. We had to force another locked steel door to get to the roof. We were above the fire and it was important to get this door open. Joe inserted the peen of his Halligan bar into the large Yale lock and leaned back with all his strength. I jumped in to help. The lock snapped and flew off the hasp with a loud twanging sound as it bounced down the stairs.

We secured the roof door and returned down the stairs to look for people. We found the top portion of the building was unoccupied. Everything above the fifth floor was empty. Suddenly the fire burst through the third floor doorway and extended into the stairwell. Like Plastic Man's arm it chased us up and out the opening to the roof. We could hear the evil woofing sound as the flames reached out to consume us. Joe was out first and I was close behind. I made a perfect diving exit losing my helmet in the process. Joe slammed the large steel door shut.

We sat for a few seconds to gather our composure. We had the hose roller and rope with us. We had an axe and one Halligan bar. We dropped our air tanks and ran to the edge of the building. Looking down we saw the flames coming from the windows on the third floor. There were hose lines stretched into the entrance of the building. We knew our guys were attacking the fire. We ran around the perimeter of the roof checking things out. We could see Ladder 12 starting to prepare a water tower at the rear of the building. This thing was going to a fifth alarm and we could hear sirens coming from every direction. Squad Four arrived on the scene and Firefighters poured out ready for action. They headed for the building entrance following the hose lines up to the seat of the fire. Another truck company was putting up as many ladders as they could. It was chaotic and graceful at the same time. It was a ballet of good and evil dancing together on a cold night in the Cass Corridor of Detroit.

We could see our rig. The boss and driver were looking up at us and waving frantically. They were yelling and pointing at the far corner of the building. We could not hear them but we directed our attention to the area they seemed so concerned about. We ran to that corner of the roof and looked down. The smoke was blowing and billowing below us. It obscured most of the building wall. A pause in the wind produced an electrifying sight. A middle aged black woman was leaning out of a window two floors up from the apartment where the arsonist had set the fire. Fire was roaring out the window next to her position. It was evident the fire was moving quickly. She had her arms extended and was holding what looked like a small baby. Even where we were, several stories above, we could hear her screams. They were the kind of screams that made you shiver.

"We got one in trouble down there and it looks like she has a baby with her," Joe said.

"Yeah the ladders can't reach her and the stairwells are blocked. She's in deep shit," I answered.

There was no time to waste. We had to get down there, somehow, to help her and the kid. All we had was the hose roller and rope.

"Make a rescue harness and tie me in. Run it to that chimney to tie it off and let's see if we can snatch them out of there," Joe yelled.

"Joe I don't know if I have the strength to lower you down four or five floors. I damn well know I don't have the strength to pull you back up," I said.

"What's the alternative Bob? If we slip when I am going down the worse that can happen is a few rope burns and a sudden stop. They have no chance at all as it now stands. Get to the edge of the building and let's go to work."

I knew he was right and I had been fashioning the rescue harness as we talked. The end of the rope now looked like something that resembled a parachute rig. It had two leg holes and an extension that went around the wearer's torso just under the arms. The knots had to be tied properly so the rope would not tighten and crush Joe when he was lowered down. These knots were even more critical when the weight of the victim is added to the load. I felt good that Joe trusted me. My main concern was the quality of the rope. Could this two inch thick line do the job? We would find out shortly.

Joe threw off his helmet and fire coat. He slipped into the harness. We moved to the chimney to make sure the end of the rope was secure. We scrambled back to the parapet of the roof. The stink and sting of the smoke filled our nostrils. Joe reached out with his gloved hand and put it behind my neck. He steadied my head and looked into my eyes.

"Let's do it Bobby," he said in a low voice.

There was no pole or post to make a double wrap to slow the lowering rope. This baby was going to take brute strength. My main concern was what Joe was going to do when he got to the window where the lady and kid were trapped. The women looked like the fat lady who sings when it's over so her weight was going to be a problem. I hoped Joe would figure it out on the way down. It was important to get them out of that room as quickly as possible. If we didn't reach them soon they would jump. Even Firefighters jump when they are on fire.

I sat on the roof and put my boots solidly against the parapet. I grabbed the rope in my gloved hands and nodded at Joe to get going. He sat for a second on the edge then turned on his stomach. He glanced at me before he went over the edge. His face telegraphed trust and determination. He clutched the rope above the knot and slowly lowered his body until I could feel his weight pulling the rope tight.

Communications was going to be a problem. I was in a sitting position leaning back against the pull of the rope. I could barely hear Joe yelling to lower him a little faster. I could not see the action. I had to rely on Joe's directions to get him into position for the rescue. Joe was moving down the outside wall through the oscillating smoke. The wind controlled the visibility. A strong gust would occasionally clear the area of the blinding smoke. Joe had picked a good point to descend. He would end up about two feet to the left of the window where the woman was leaning out screaming.

As he neared his target he shouted orders to the fat lady. I could still hear Joe but the distance was making his voice fade in and out.

"Keep going Bobby," he yelled.

He told the woman he was going to swing into the window to assist her. He knew from experience that this would be the most dangerous time of the rescue attempt. People who are trapped will sometimes lunge for their rescuers with fatal results.

Joe told the woman to step back to the side of the window.

"Stop Bobby," he shouted.

I could not see him but could feel his next action. Leaning back against the harness he swung inward and pushed off the wall with both feet. He swung out and away in an arc then came rushing back toward the wall. He disappeared into the window like a shell sliding into the breech of a cannon.

He was on his feet quickly and removed his harness. The woman's eyes were glazed with fear. Tears were running down her cheeks and snot hung from her nose in long dirty strings. She clutched the screaming crying baby to her bosom. Joe grabbed the woman by the shoulders and gave her instructions.

"It is important you listen to me and do what I say. Do you understand?"

She continued blubbering but nodded her head indicating she understood. As the smoke and heat swirled around them Joe slipped the harness up her legs and secured it to her body. She held the baby away from her body as Joe hooked her up. The Little guy was squirming and kicking both of them. It was a crazy scene but things were going the way Joe had planned them. Joe positioned the woman in a sitting position on the sill high above the Cass Corridor.

He leaned out the window and shouted to me," She's coming out Bobby. Start lowering the rope."

Ladder Eight is an eighty five foot aerial apparatus. The men manning the rig had positioned it directly in front of the building. They extended the ladder as far as it could reach. They were hampered by the cars parked at the curb. The end of the ladder was one story short of where the woman was trapped. Two Firefighters were at the top watching the unfolding drama above them.

Joe gently slid the woman and her child over the edge. The rope tightened under the weight of their bodies. Joe yelled again for me to start lowering them down. It went smoothly. The men waiting at the top of the ladder reached out and pulled them in. They safely descended with one man assisting the lady and the other carrying the squalling kicking child. I returned the rope for Joe and shortly after he and I came down the same route.

Moments later, when we were all on the ground, the fire boiled out the window and caught the rope on fire. We watched as it burned like the fuse on a fire cracker. Joe looked at me and we both smiled. We were young and danger was a part of our game.

Not all rescues work that smoothly. The attempts we were making tonight at Cheboygan Community hospital would test every bit of knowledge and experience we possessed.

Chapter Thirteen

Officer Kelly remained with his trapped partner. They donned the air tanks rescuers handed up to them. It was good to breathe pure air again. The tearing and blurring of their eyes stopped. The heat was uncomfortable but still tolerable. Kelly was vigorously swinging his eight pound sledge hammer. He worked from the edge of the escape hole toward the area where his friend's foot was caught in the floor fissure.

Mel couldn't move. He was glad he had wedged the two by four into the opening. His foot was numb from the pressure but at least it had not been severed by the weight of the settling building. He continued to work feverishly to keep the area around his leg open. Kelly kept chipping away at the floor.

Outside Borza regained a bit of his strength. He was a powerfully built man with sloping shoulders. He reached down with his one good hand and pulled Chum to his feet.

"We have to get back into the building. Think you can make it?"

"Yeah, I guess I'm done puking. I can see why they call you guys smoke eaters. This stuff tastes like shit. Let's go."

They headed back into the building.

Mel could hear the guys working below him. The whine and crunching sound of the partner saw filled the area with an ear throbbing roar. The sound promised rescue and safety. Mel had been in tough spots before. His experiences in Viet Nam put him in harms way many times. Death came suddenly in Nam. His present situation promised a slow painful death. Only the commitment of the men working around him could resolve his predicament. He could feel the room getting hotter and he was drenched in sweat. He had a cold fear of not being able to get his foot free. His life was in the hands of others. It was a helpless feeling for such a strong man.

On the first floor Pierce climbed up on the desk and relieved Barkley. He completed the arc shaped cut connecting the crack in two places. He expected it to drop like a scroll saw cutting a piece of plywood. It did not happen. The blade of the saw was unable to cut deep enough to reach the rebar reinforcing the concrete ceiling. Pierce felt the hands of Borza and Chum on his legs as they groped their way through the darkness returning to where Mel was trapped.

He stood on his tip toes and peered into the crack. His flashlight exposed gleaming metal. The saw blade had cut the rebar about half way through. He restarted the saw and tried again. His saw could not reach the rebar.

"It's going to be bull work from here on," he yelled to those below.

Pierce was the reason we were here tonight. He had thrown a great wedding for his grand daughter. The Firefighters he invited were retired. They had been the cream of the Detroit Fire Department when they were on the job. If you had to pick a crew to fight a fire it would be this gang.

In our working years we knew Mac Pierce to be a tough smart Firefighter. His time with Squad Four enriched him with knowledge and experience. We trusted his judgment. When he told us it was going to be bull work we knew we had a tough task ahead of us. He dropped the now useless partner saw. It made a clunk clank sound as it bounced off the desk and hit the floor.

"Give me that Halligan bar and one of you jump up here and give me a hand," Pierce shouted.

Borza helped Chum struggle to the desk top to assist Pierce.

The surface on the end of the Halligan bar is shaped like a thick forked wedge. With this part inserted in the crack both men pulled down with all their strength. They grunted and groaned as they put every once of energy into the task.

"Shit it ain't happening. We need more leverage. Get up here and help," Pierce shouted.

"I can't help with one fricken arm. I'm going back to help Danny. He is alone on the line." Borza answered as he stumbled back toward the fire.

Danny had been forced to retreat another four or five feet by the advancing flames. The fire was trying to reach the open doorway. It would reach out with an occasional tongue of flame to taste the fresh oxygen. Danny knew he was fighting a monster that meant to kill us all.

Borza's instincts told him to leave as he passed the open doorway moving back toward the fire. His commitment to his friends killed that impulse. He stumbled and scrambled back and was soon next to Danny backing him up.

Barkley jumped on top of the desk to help the struggling men. He jammed his bar into the crack and wrapped his big hands around the tool and heaved. He thought he felt a slight movement.

Again fate intervened. The roaring fire on the first floor managed to burn through a closet door at the rear of the building. The closet contained several more propane tanks. Careless staff members had been too lazy to take the tanks to a proper storing area outside the building. The paint on the tanks started to blister and melt as the temperature on their surfaces increased. The gases inside started to boil and expand. The noise started with a low whistle then built to a louder hissing and eventually to a screaming howl.

The noise was hideous and added stress to the men working in the corridor.

Officer Kelly paused with the sledge in his hand and said," Holy crap it sounds like something else is getting ready to blow. Don't stop guys. That's the same sound we heard just before the building blew up the last time."

Mel reached over to grab Kelly's arm and said, "Give me the sledge and drop down and help those guys below. They need more leverage."

"No. I'm staying with you. I'm going to see it through until we get you out of here."

The efforts of the men started to pay off. The water flow increased as the Halligan bars widened the crack.

"Pull damn it pull," Mac Pierce hollered.

The men grunted, gasped, and strained as they attempted to pry the concrete loose. Barkley was actually hanging on his tool like an athlete doing chin ups. He would drag his body up a few inches and let it drop with a repeated jerking motion. Chum had one foot on the desk and the other on the wall to increase his leverage. Ever so slowly the ceiling started to give. They only had to move the wedge a few inches to free the trapped officer. It was over in an instant. The floor opened up. The two by four placed in the crack to protect the policeman's ankle came crashing down like a guillotine. It made a distinctive smack crack sound as it landed on top of Chum Dupree's foot. The force of the dropping plank split the nail of Chum's big toe and broke the bone.

With a yowl of pain Chum fell against Pierce and Barkley knocking them from the desk. There was a crashing clattering sound as all three men went down. Their tools sounded like dueling sabers as they hit each other when they fell. The hallway was full of noise mixed with cursing and yelling.

Chum was holding his foot shouting, "Oh shit. Oh shit."

Pierce was struggling to get up and Barkley was trying to shake the cob webs from his head. Above them they could hear the two policemen moving to the opening and freedom.

The blackness of the smoke hid all this action even from those who were standing next to each other. Down the hall

Danny was fighting the nozzle which seemed to be gathering strength by the minute. The water pressure felt like it was rising. Danny wondered if Bobby Kazoo was watching his gauges.

Danny yelled back down the corridor, "What the hell are you guys doing back there? We ain't got time to waste. Let's get with it.

"We got em Danny. We're headed out."

The two policemen dropped down and headed for the side door and freedom. Pierce was leading the way with his left hand on the wall. Danny's voice gave him direction. The two cops were right behind Pierce. Mel Dupree was hopping on one foot. Officer Kelly was supporting him with an arm around his waist. Mel had no feeling in his foot. The circulation had been cut off by being wedged in the floor. He had a big smile on his face that no one could see. His only concern was to get out before another explosion occurred.

Next in line was Chum. He was clutching the back of Kelly's shirt. He had his head down and was also hopping on one foot. The pain in his big toe was maddening. He continued to curse with every jarring hop. Barkley was last in line. He gathered up the tools and helped escort the injured men out of the building. He knew he would have to go back in to help Danny. The most important task now facing this fire crew was to get to those venting propane tanks before they exploded.

"Let's get these guys out and bring in a couple of inch and a half lines to help Danny," Pierce called back to Barkley.

"Sounds good to me. We can handle the smaller lines easier and maybe take back some of the ground we lost to this fricken fire."

Pierce led the rag tag group to the exit doorway. He slipped out and turned to help the others as they exited the building. Out came the Dupree brothers. Both men were hopping on one foot. They supported each other as they moved. From where Bobby Kazoo was standing, working the fire rigs, it looked like a potato bag race. Kelly popped out and then came Barkley.

Bobby Kazoo smiled. His running mates were safe. They successfully rescued the cops. He was proud of them but knew there was a bigger job ahead. Those kids were still trapped on the fifth floor. It would be difficult to get them out. He knew there was a stalemate between the fire and Danny on the first floor. The fire on the upper floors was moving rapidly. Bobby could see the fire had already moved into every room. This meant that Joe and his guys would be cut off from returning down the stairwell once they made it to the fifth floor IC unit room.

When they got to Bobby the survivors sat on the running board of the rig. Pierce let out a gasp as his back muscles started to cramp. He crumpled to the ground in pain. He was through for the night. He could not help Barkley going back in to help Danny.

The casualty list was growing. The watchman was missing and most likely dead. The two cops nearly lost their lives. The cost of getting them out had put Lee Long in the hospital and now Pierce was out of action. Both cops were injured and Borza was hurt and bleeding. The unofficial toll was five injured and possibly one fatality. Bobby had a bad feeling that this fire would wreak more havoc before it was brought under control.

The closest analogy Bobby's could think of was the warehouse fire behind the training academy in 1980. Most of the men fighting the fire tonight had been at that tragic fifth alarm. The call came in about two in the afternoon. Arriving fire companies could see wisps of smoke coming out the upper floor windows. It was an abandoned warehouse that occupied an entire city block. Buildings like this were used by homeless people for shelter. When it was cold they would build fires on the floor to keep warm. A call like this usually involved a search for the fire and extinguishment with the light red line.

There were three engines, two ladder units, a squad, and a chief assigned to this box alarm. The arriving Firefighters moved up to the third floor and spread out to look for the fire. Most of these old warehouses had the same building construction. There were well worn wooden floors and large rooms with high ceilings. Each room was encircled with a three foot overhang that could trap large volumes of rising smoke. The smoke moved from room to room filling these bays with volatile gas and fumes. The searching Firefighters had no idea that every bay on the fire floor had filled with smoke. The wisps of smoke seen from the street gave no indication of the pending danger. The hot gasses trapped in the bays were a growing time bomb.

The original fire was started in a pile of trash. This time it was not a bum who started a fire to keep warm. It was an arsonist who set fires for thrills. He was smart and started the blaze at the rear of the building on the third floor. The fire grew in size as the smoke extended through rooms and hallways looking for oxygen to fuel its hungry appetite.

It happened in a flash. The hot gases seeping out the front windows sucked in fresh oxygen and sent it to the fire at the rear of the warehouse. The blazing pile of trash inhaled the oxygen and raised the fire temperature a degree or two. The small temperature rise was enough to ignite all the accumulated smoke and gasses in the building. The men were caught in a giant rolling fire ball. They turned and ran for their lives.

Several Firefighters were able to make the stairwell and tumbled over each other as they fell down the stairs. They were the lucky ones. Others could barely make it to the windows where the fire was venting itself. Instantaneous choices had to be made. As the fire roared out the windows many Firefighters were forced to jump. Bobby was standing next to his rig and watched in horror.

The first man to jump did not hesitate. He threw his axe out and jumped for safety. He came down with his arms extended for balance and hit the wires feeding electricity to the building. He spun in a half circle and crashed to the ground. The contact with the wire ripped open his fire coat and he sustained a slashing cut to his arm. He hit the ground with a sickening thud but was alive and safe,

Two others made it to a window but did not jump. They were hanging out the window holding on to the sill. They screamed for help. Another Firefighter was hanging out a window closer to where a huge volume of fire was venting. Bobby Kazoo saw the fire roll over the man's hands forcing him to let go. He was the first to perish at this fire. Bobby leaped to the top side of his rig and directed the monitor gun at the fire above the dangling firefighters. Other men took a ladder from his rig and were able to reach the two firefighters still hanging on.

There was more tragedy to come at this fire scene. The arriving chief asked for more help and it eventually became a 5th alarm. As darkness fell the fire crews were starting to get the upper hand. Several units had worked their way into the warehouse and were pushing the flames into an ever shrinking circle.

The Lieutenant in charge of an arriving relief company took his rookie trial man into an area near the seat of the fire. It was a spot where the fire had burned through several floors and out the roof. It was dark but the men could see the night sky when they looked up. Joe Barchilli was helping them.

The Lieutenant turned to Joe and asked him to go back and pull the line so they could move forward. Joe scrambled to a doorway where the line was hung up. As Joe bent over to grab the line he heard a tremendous crashing sound. The sound ended with a whomping thud and the air was filled with dust and ash. Joe wheeled around and his eyes followed the line back to where he had been working with the fire crew. His heart ached at what he saw. The hose line ended at a gapping hole in the floor that was filled with the debris of a collapsed wall. His mates were gone. Silence filled the area. Joe was alone. He realized that fate had just spared him from a crushing death.

Tonight at the hospital fire in Cheboygan Bobby thought of the warehouse fire and the "what if factor." What if they had been minutes earlier or later at that fire? What if Joe had not been sent back to pull line? What if they had not been in town tonight attending the wedding? It puzzled Bobby why some survived and some perished. He said a silent prayer for his friends and hoped they would survive this night. He knew because of the "what if factor" those kids trapped in this fire were going to at least have a chance to be rescued by his friends.

Chapter Fourteen

The governor meant well when he sent the fire units to the emergency at the University. The fire was threatening the library where some of the rarest books in the world were stored. Even some of Hemingway's notes and papers were stored there. The library was an important part of the history and heritage of the University. The Governor didn't realize the risk he was taking when he ordered every fire unit in a fifty mile radius to respond. He violated a golden rule of emergency services. He had no reserve units on stand by.

Fighting a fire is similar to fighting a war. Tactics and procedures are executed in a military manner. Committing all your forces in a battle is risky. A disaster can result from an all or nothing decision. Leaders must listen to their generals. History is riddled with examples of politicians not listening to the professionals. Decisions that risk lives demand the consul of experts.

Many times rescuers must be rescued themselves. The fire we were fighting tonight was an example of that situation. The Governor's decision to drain fire protection from the Cheboygan area put the entire area at risk. We had no backup available at the hospital fire. We were on our own. We were irreversibly committed. There would be no one to rescue the rescuers.

When the Governor learned of the pending disaster in Cheboygan he begin to listen to his experts. One of the Governor's aides was a former Deputy Chief of the Lansing Fire Department. His present position was Director of Emergency Services for the State of Michigan. He was furious. His first priority was to get an accurate overview of the situation. He contacted the Cheboygan 911 operator. The dispatcher gave an update on the hospital fire.

She said, "The fire is growing in magnitude. The watchman is missing. A nurse and some children are trapped on the fifth floor. A team of retired Firefighters volunteered their services and are now working at the fire. They are attempting to rescue the trapped victims. We are not in contact with the rescue team and are not able to monitor their progress. One Firefighter has been taken to a medical facility for treatments and an EMS unit is presently transporting two injured police officers to a medical facility."

The director made a quick assessment. On the positive side the fire at the library was starting to come under control. It looked like they were going to be able to save most of the rare books stored at the facility. The negative side was the fire in Cheboygan. He dispatched the fastest apparatus back to the hospital fire. Help was on the way. Would they get there in time?

The crowd watching the fire in Cheboygan was anxious. Everyone was aware the children were trapped inside. Lulu's mother was petrified as she stared at the intensive care unit window on the fifth floor. She could see flames coming from windows on the lower floors. The fire seemed to be making steady progress toward the area where her little girl was trapped. Her stress was compounded when informed her son Billy was with the rescue team attempting to reach Lulu. There was a chance she could lose all her children in this fire. Her eyes remained fixed on the window and she started to cry.

The women at the Cheboygan Fire station were getting nervous. They heard the radio report given to the Director of Emergency Services. News that the rescue team was not communicating was disconcerting. The women could contain themselves no longer.

"We have to go to the fire," one of them said.

Bobby Kazoo's wife answered, "You're right. I can't stand waiting here anymore. We can find Bobby and maybe help him. It's not time to sit on our asses in this darn fire station."

She asked the police officer, who had just returned from the hospital, to take them to the fire.

"You're damned right I will. I can't stand the wait either. I got buddies involved in this thing. Let's get rolling ladies."

They hurried out the door to the squad car. The flashers threw a circle of blue and white light into the cool night air. Roosting birds sitting in the trees near the station were startled. A raccoon looking for food stared blankly at the squad car. His eyes reflected like two laser beams in the darkness. The lights were joined by the piercing sound of the siren as the black patrol car powered its way toward the fire. The raccoon slipped to the far side of the tree. He could care less about what was going on. The women looked toward the end of town where the fire was illuminating the night sky. They intended to get involved in the action.

At the fire Bobby Kazoo organized a group of volunteers. He put them to work setting up hoses and they were now pouring water into the rear of the building. He created a command post close to his working pumpers. He directed all arriving EMS ambulances and police cars to a spot behind the fire engines. A state police commander on the scene set up a communications center. There was now a coordinated connection between the police, the dispatcher, EMS units and Bobby. The only people not connected were the Firefighters in the building.

Bobby was relying on his fire fighting knowledge to help those inside the burning building. He was working as many hose lines as his pumpers could safely supply. The condition of the rigs pleased him. The volunteer department had done a good job of maintaining these old machines. The Ahrens Fox dated back to the 1920s and the Seagrave J-Model was from the early 1930s. They were both purring like contented kittens.

The police commander informed Bobby that help was on the way. It would be at least forty five minutes before they arrived on the scene. A group of men milled around the command post waiting to help. Bobby ordered them to gather all the ladders they could find and place them close to the burning building. Bobby reasoned that if any of the trapped victims could get to a window the men would be able to get a ladder up quickly to reach them. Bobby knew there was no ladder long enough to reach the fifth floor.

Joe will get to them and figure it out he thought. Over the years he had seen Joe display an amazing resourcefulness at fire scenes. Joe earned the admiration of his co-workers from his first day at the academy until the day he retired as a Deputy Chief. That was a span of thirty years and here we were still depending on Joe.

Chapter Fifteen

Bobby, Danny and I had been in Joe's class at the training academy. We all hired in at the same time. We were pumped up that first day. It was a boot camp for Firefighters. We met our instructors for the first time and they made a lasting impression on us. We called our head instructor Captain Boomer. This was not his real name but it was an appropriate handle for a guy who could be heard a mile away when he yelled. I swear the first time he shouted at us he blew the hats off everyone standing in the front rank of our morning formation. Joe told me he saw two mice running out the open apparatus room doors of the academy in fear for their lives. This guy was a throw back to the days when they used voice communication at fires. If he yelled fore playing golf everyone on the entire course ducked and birds would fly out of the trees. He was a good instructor but he scared the hell out of us. He was particularly hard on Joe because Joe was our unnamed leader. Joe never backed down from anything.

We were exposed to tasks that tested our courage. The Pompier ladder was our first challenge. The inside of the academy was like an enormous gymnasium. There was a five story wall that simulated the outside of an office or apartment building. Captain Boomer ordered us to scale this wall using the Pompier ladder. Joe stepped forward and said he would go first.

The Pompier is a device that looks like a twelve foot rail with a large hook on the top and peg like steps to climb on. It is a two man process to use this ladder. The first man will start by reaching out and hooking the ladder into the window of the next floor up. The second man will hold the bottom of the rail while the first man starts up. After getting to the top the man will enter the window and wait for his partner. The process is repeated and the Firefighters can climb any building that has windows. It is a very scary ladder to climb. Joe took Bobby with him. When they got to the top Joe leaned out and waved..

Our confidence rose as we trained and we got used to Captain Boomer's yelling. I think even the mice moved back in after a few weeks. We were taught that an interior attack was the most effective way to fight a fire. We learned the chemistry of fire and how removing any side of the fire triangle extinguished the flames. Our instructors gave us the basics of hydraulics and showed us how friction loss affected water moving through hose lines. There were many skills to master and as we learned there is no substitute for on the job experience. Captain Boomer promised to take us to a staged fire before we graduated. The purpose of the exercise was to demonstrate fire tactics. Captain Boomer and Lieutenant Calmly would set a fire in an abandoned dwelling and give us instruction on how to put the fire out.

Lieutenant Calmly was not his real name. We hung that title on him because of the stark contrast between the two instructors. Boomer was like a super hero to us cadets. He was a tall man. He stood six feet tall and reminded you of a military first sergeant. He looked like he was always standing at attention. He was ram rod straight and his eyes could glare at you like a tank flame thrower. Most of the upper echelon officers in the department at that time were World War Two or Korean Police Action veterans. Boomer had been a Marine. He participated in the assaults on

Tarawa, Pelelu, and Saipan. His demeanor and body language reflected his years in the Corps.

Lieutenant Calmly was an exact opposite of Boomer. He was shorter and had drooping shoulders. His face had a bland expression with blank eyes that seemed to see nothing. His hair was a mixture of black and gray. His personality had a milk toast demeanor. Both Boomer and Calmly sported brush haircuts with no sideburns. When Boomer was dressing us down for some goof up or error I would peek at Calmly and see that dead pan expression. There were times when I could almost see a smile trying to turn the corner of his lips. It was as if he was enjoying our misery.

After a few weeks at the academy we learned we could confide in Lt. Calmly. He would sympathize with our complaints and fears. We were too young and inexperienced to know this was all part of the program. They were able to find out our concerns and work on building our confidence. They were also able to identify who would make the grade and who would wash out.

The day finally came when our instructors took us to the staged fire they had promised. We climbed aboard our academy fire apparatus and headed for the house we were going to set on fire. There were 30 of us piled on top and hanging off the sides of the old fire engine. We must have looked like a clown team heading to the circus. People paused to stare as we passed them by. It was a nice fall day and the sunshine reflected off the polished metal and chrome of our rig. Our training officers wore dress uniforms. They sat straight and tall in the front seat with Captain Boomer driving the ancient apparatus.

There was a section of run down turn of the century houses on a street behind the academy. The buildings were close together and two stories high. Each had a first floor living area with bedrooms upstairs. The city was clearing this area for a new expressway.

They were in the process of demolishing them in preparation for the construction crews. Some houses were still occupied but most were empty. Windows in the empty ones had been broken by kids roaming the neighborhood. Vagrants and street people used some of the dwellings for shelter. This was once been a thriving prosperous community. Each house had a story to tell. The love and laughter that once filled these homes had long ago drifted into the annuals of time. All that remained was the silence of despair and an aura of poverty. These houses would soon be victims of city bulldozers. On this day one of them was going to go up in flames.

We turned onto one of the streets. Captain Boomer slowed the fire engine to a crawl. He stopped in the middle of the block and looked at a likely prospect. He and his assistant, Lt. calmly, walked into the old dwelling. A few cadets sat atop the hose bed of the ancient pumper while the rest of the class stood around looking up at the old house. The sun was shining and we were enjoying a peaceful break from our training schedule.

The afternoon suddenly turned into an action filled nightmare. We heard a bellowing and shouting coming from the building. There was the thunder of footsteps that sounded like a football team running down a stairway. Everybody's heart skipped a beat when Captain Boomer came crashing out the front door. He knocked the door completely off its hinges.

He was yelling, "Let's go guys. We have a working fire going in the attic and we have to put it out now. Get your god damn gear on and make sure your masks are operating. Let's go. Let's go."

The men on top of the rig were on the ground in an instant. Those who were walking around sprang into action. A few cadets ran into each other as they scrambled to get into their turnout gear. Lt. Calmly grabbed two cadets and put them in the front seat of the apparatus. They were going to help him hook up to the hydrant. The men were quickly dressed and ready for action.

Smoke was starting to come out of the second floor windows. Captain Boomer ordered us to stretch two lines from the engine to the front porch. He said," Break open the hose bundles and put on your masks. I want you to spread out the lines so they won't kink when we get water."

He ordered the backup line to be placed the front porch near the door.

Then Captain Boomer made a mistake. He took six of us, including his star pupil Joe, into the building with a dry line. We went up a winding stairway into a bedroom then up a small ladder through a shuttle hole into a smoky attic. We dragged the empty hose all the way up, over, and around all obstacles. We were ready to fight our first fire. Everyone was lying on the floor of the attic. Our instructors had set a fire in a piss soaked mattress. The mattress was emitting huge volumes of ugly black smoke. We could hear the rig outside as it took off looking for a fire hydrant. There was an uneasy silence. We waited.

Our excitement grew as the smoke started to fill the attic. You could hear the sucking sounds of our masks as our lungs demanded air. We sounded like a group of Darth Vader impersonators. The Captain was near the cadets who were lying on the floor. He was on the ladder with just his head extended into the attic. From this position he could supervise and give commands without taking a beating from the fire. We waited.

We watched as the smoldering fire turned the mattress into a roaring blaze that extended to the roof boards. We watched as the fire reached the peak of the room and spread out in two directions looking for oxygen. We waited.

We felt the heat build up in our confined space. The thick smoke descended around us until we could not see the man next to us.

We heard Captain Boomer yell," Where the fuck is the water?"

We waited.

The fire department axiom of when one thing turns to shit everything turns to shit was now starting to occur. Lt. Calmly and his men had revved their old rig and headed for a hydrant to deliver water to the burning attic. The line peeled off the back of the apparatus smoothly. Soon there was

114

several hundred feet of dry line extending from the back of the rig to the seat of the fire. The first hydrant was over a block away. Lieutenant Calmly nosed the pumper into the red and yellow fire plug and the cadets sprang into action.

One of the men placed a wrench on the opening nut at the top of the hydrant then tried to remove the cap covers by hand to hook up the pumper's soft suction. He struggled a few moments then put the wrench on one of the caps and kicked hard with his booted foot. Off came the cap and out fell a piece of ice. Peering into the opening he could see the hydrant was frozen solid. It was early fall and there had been several nights with below freezing temperatures. Apparently this district of hydrants had not been checked by the nearest fire company.

Precious minutes were being lost. Mistakes were now being compounded. Everything was turning to shit. Our instructors were good men but had become careless. They failed to check for a working hydrant before starting the fire. They had taken Firefighters into a burning building without a charged hose line and worst of all they had no back up. The turn to shit scenario was in full bloom and escalating.

The men on the pumper had to reattach the hose line to the fire engine hose bed. They clambered back onto the rig and moved on to find another hydrant. Lt. Calmly floored the old Seagrave. He was moving as fast as he could while watching the line peel off the apparatus through his rear view mirror. The block ended and he turned the corner to move to the next street. He prayed that he could find a working hydrant. The rig was still moving when it ran out of line. Both hose beds had been emptied and they were still a hundred feet from the next fire hydrant. To make matters worse there was no radio on the rig and in the early 1960s there was no hand held communications. There was no way to call for help.

Those of us who were lying on the floor of the attic with the fire raging around us were thinking the same thoughts. We wondered if all fires were like this. We wondered if we were strong enough to stand up to this kind of pounding and we wondered if Captain Boomer was trying to kill us. Joe was on the pipe. He was leading as usual. This was our first encounter with the fire dragon and it was scary. It had a thousand tongues trying to reach us. Joe had his head down and shoulders hunched facing the flames. I could hear him cursing and I knew he was gritting his teeth.

Suddenly Captain Boomer shouted, "Everyone out. Leave the fucking line and get your asses out of here."

He didn't have to say it twice. Before the Captain could get off the ladder we ran over him. I think I stepped on his hand as I headed out. The building was filled with the sounds of panic. There was cursing and the thunder of booted feet racing down the stairwell. Helmets were clattering as they fell from heads and were kicked with other debris strewn along the stairs. The first person to the door fell and the rest of us tumbled over him. The Captain was out last and bellowing louder than any of us had ever heard him. I truly believe those mice several blocks away vacated the academy again. Captain Boomer stood on the porch and vented his rage in a language we could not understand. It sounded like he was speaking in tongues. On that cool fall day I believe his image could have replaced the MGM lion.

We turned to look at the house we had just bailed out of. The fire broke through the roof and black smoke billowed into the sky. Passers by saw the smoke and sent an alarm through a corner call box. We could hear the sirens in the distance on the way to our location. We stood by silently as Captain Boomer took a head count to make sure we were all out. Meanwhile Lt. calmly was starting to get control of our fire problem. He checked the compartments on his rig and found several rolls of two and a half inch line. He ordered his helpers to hook these lines to the end of the 1500 feet of line that led back to the fire. Luckily the hose was long enough to reach the engine that was hooked to a working hydrant. The cadet at the hydrant opened the valve and started to supply water to Captain Boomer and his Firefighters.

Joe and a couple of guys re-entered the burning house to pull the hose out before it burned up. Joe went to the first landing of the stairwell and was able to get the line down.

He grabbed the nozzle and walked out onto the porch. He put it down next to the second line. Both nozzles were unknowingly left in the open position as Joe walked away.

Water from Lt. calmly's hydrant reached the nozzles about the same time as fire companies were arriving on the scene. The lines lying on the porch turned into lively jumping snakes. The pressure supplied by the pumper energized the hoses and they launched an assault on anyone standing near them. They lashed and jumped like Zorro's whip. One line spun in a half arc and hit the Captain on the knee. He went down like wheat being cut by a scythe. The cadets sprang into action. They jumped on the hoses and pinned them to the ground. Joe stood up with one of the pipes under his control. I was standing behind him. We were ready to go back in and fight the fire.

Squad Four was the first arriving company. These men were the elite of the west side. They came out of the rig in a grumpy mood and glared at the rookies standing around.

It was afternoon and they had been enjoying a mid day nap. To be sent to help correct some screw up by the trainees from the academy pissed them off. The moment they were out in the open Joe turned to straighten out his line. Joe accidentally directed his fully discharging pipe into the members of Squad Four. He blew off their helmets and knocked them down. They were soaked with water and their lieutenant had his cigar knocked from his mouth. New cuss words were invented that day and lessons were learned. It was an auspicious start for the class of 1962.

After eight weeks we were ready for graduation. Joe was number one in our class. He received the first of the many decorations he would accumulate during his time on the department. At the graduation the cadets gave demonstrations of our skills. Joe had developed a spectacular way to exit a building. He would dive head first out the fifth floor window of the academy wall and plunge several floors before he engaged the brake knot he tied in his safety line. The crowd gasped in astonishment and loudly applauded the feat. We were proud of Joe. He made us all look good that day.

Chapter Sixteen

The police car wheeled into the hospital parking lot. The blue and white flashers were still spinning as the girls stepped out of the vehicle. Bobby caught his wife in his arms and swung her around.

He put his face near her ear and said," I love you baby. How are you girls holding up?"

"Oh Bobby, we just couldn't stay at the fire hall. We were worried to death about you guys."

Bobby turned his wife around so they were both facing the women.

He spoke in a loud voice, "I'm not going to kid you. The guys are in a dangerous situation. Joe, Bob, and Carl are somewhere above the fire. They took a big kid with them to help with the bull work. They're going to move down the fifth floor hallway to reach those trapped kids. If they can make it they will probably try to bring them out the window. The bad news is we don't have a ladder that can reach the fifth floor."

The girls started to talk at the same time. They were frightened and stressed.

Carl's wife asked, "Is there any other way out? How about going to the roof?"

"The roof won't work because the stairwells are turning into chimneys full of fire. Their only chance is to get into the

119

room and bring everyone down the outside of the building from the window."

They turned to stare at the hospital where the fire was rapidly expanding. Huge volumes of smoke filled the northern Michigan sky. People standing around the fire were illuminated by the flames. The men working the hoses near the rear of the building were taking a beating from the radiant heat. The men bent low and turned their faces away from the blaze.

A portion of the back wall suddenly collapsed with a crashing roar. The ground quaked as tons of bricks and debris came smashing down to earth. Ashes and sparks soared skyward and blended into the growing smoke column. The men manning the hoses dropped their nozzles and ran. They returned when they realized the wall had fallen away from their position

The high-pitched screeching of the superheated propane tanks added to the tension at the scene. The falling wall had sent a gust of air rushing into the corridor where the fire suppression team was making a stand. A blast of hot air and flames rolled over the men and drove them to the floor. There was a sucking sound as the fire swirled back to its original position.

Danny was whipping the line around in a circular motion to drive the fire back. He was cussing and yelling loudly. He was pissed off.

"This is bullshit. We better get some help or this fire is going to beat us."

Borza slipped outside to hook up another line. He moved as fast as his aching body could carry him to reenter the hallway. It was difficult because of the deep cut on his arm. He was working with one hand. He looked at the tourniquet and saw it was soaked through with blood. He was hurting and starting to get light headed. Still he slipped on his mask and dragged the hose into the fray. He stumbled down the hallway and collapsed next to Danny and Barkley. He yelled in Danny's ear to take the second line because he couldn't manage it alone.

"We got it," Danny answered.

They sat huddled together pouring tons of water into the blazing hallway. Slowly the tide of battle started to change. With the entire back of the building gone the fire began to take another direction. The flames were seeking oxygen and used the path of least resistance. Danny and his crew could sense the change in the situation.

Danny said, "Everybody up. Let's start pushing this bastard back. We got to get in a position to start cooling those propane tanks. "

They got to their feet and stood facing the fire. The two pipemen were shoulder to shoulder with Borza directly behind them. Borza was leaning into them to help fight the pressure of the water. They started to move forward a foot at a time in a shuffling manner.

The sound of the superheated tanks was hideous. The men didn't know exactly where the tanks were but the sound was easy to locate. All they had to do was keep moving toward potential disaster and hope they could get there before an explosion occurred. To say this was a dangerous situation would be an understatement. This was one of those times when you shot the dice and hoped for a good outcome. It was important to get to those tanks quickly. If the tanks exploded they would not only kill Danny and his guys but would probably take out Joe, the rescue team, and the kids trapped on the fifth floor.

They moved forward another few steps. The fire rolled back and surged forward again. The men held their ground. Danny was hurting. They were all hurting. They had sustained burns, their muscles were aching and they were winded. Without warning, Borza went down. He fell against the legs of the pipemen. Without Borza's support Danny and Barkley staggered back and nearly fell themselves.

Barkley reached down and rolled Borza over. He noticed the blood soaked tourniquet. "Danny this guy is in bad shape. We got to get him out of here. I think he is bleeding to death. Look at his arm."

"We haven't got a lot of time here. Taking him out will keep us from getting to those tanks a little longer. What do you think?" Danny asked.

"Well we can't let him die. Do you think you can hold this position while I drag him out of here?"

"Yeah I can do it if you don't take too long. Get your ass moving and take this old guy outside where he can get some help."

"Be right back," Barkley answered as he shut down his line and dropped it on the floor next to Danny.

Moving Borza's body was hard. Barkley struggled to turn the prone Firefighter in a way where his head was pointing toward the door. It would be a twenty or thirty foot drag. Barkley grabbed Borza's good arm and started pulling. He used all his weight in a lunging backward motion. He repeated this action over and over again. He was moving only a couple of feet at a time but was making progress. As he got closer to the door he called for the men outside to help him. During this time the fire was beginning to push Danny backwards again. The sound of the venting propane tanks seemed to escalate another octave.

The men outside heard Barkley hollering for help and rushed to the doorway. They were on there knees trying to get below the smoke that was pouring out of the opening. Barkley was about six feet from the door when one of the men lunged in to help him. They quickly exited the building. They were coughing and gagging from the smoke.

"Get him some help. I have to go back inside," Barkley ordered.

The women and the paramedics came running and arrived at the same time. Borza was picked up and hustled to a waiting ambulance. They took his vitals and administered oxygen. Two of the women followed Borza's wife into the emergency vehicle. They were off to the hospital.

Borza looked like he had been in a war. He was streaked with sweat. He had dirt and grime all over him. His arm was dripping blood on the floor of the ambulance. The medic cut through the tourniquet. He ripped off the sleeve of Borza's

122

shirt and poured antiseptic onto the wound. He applied a compress over the cut and added a clean bandage to complete the first aid procedure.

The women were worried but kept their composure. They helped the medics and Borza began to come around. They would be at the clinic in minutes. Borza mumbled he wanted a better room than Lee Long or the cops. His wife started to cry and kissed him on the cheek. She knew he was going to be all right.

Barkley returned to Danny's side. It was going to be tougher now. They didn't have a back up man to support them. The sound was deafening as they stood shoulder to shoulder to advance the hose lines. They were almost to the rear of the building when they discovered a side hallway. The high-pitched wail of the venting tanks was coming from the far end of the side hallway. Through the smoke they could barely make out a door. They kept moving and slowly rolled the angry fire backwards.

They finally made it to the hall door. They had to be careful they didn't get cut off by the fire. Once they moved around the corner and down this corridor there was a chance the fire could seal off their escape route. If they didn't get to those tanks it wouldn't make a difference anyhow. They had to cool those tanks to prevent an explosion. The rescue team was relying on them to hold things together. They were buying time. Danny kept looking back over his shoulder. He could see flames extending past the corner they had just turned. He would whip his line in that direction every now and then to impede the extending fire.

They reached the door and Barkley carefully pulled it open. They found a cherry red tank howling to explode. The noise was starting to hurt their ears. They blasted the time bomb with water. It hissed and spit but continued to vent pressurized gas. The tank was starting to cool but as they looked deeper into the storage area they saw the back wall of the closet was gone. Apparently when part of the rear wall of the building collapsed it took a portion of the floor on this level with it.

"Damn it Barkley this tank is cooling but I can hear another tank somewhere that sounds like it is ready to go off," Danny said.

"Yeah me too, that closet floor looks like it fell into the basement. Maybe there is another tank down there."

"Can you see over the edge?" Danny asked.

"I'll try."

Dragging his line with him, in case the floor collapsed, he moved slowly forward. He peered over the edge into a smoky spark filled nightmare. It was a mess of shattered wood and plaster. He could hear the tank but could not see it.

"Without going down there the best we can do is shoot water into the basement and hope we can hit the tank to cool it," Barkley said.

"We're not in a very good spot here," Danny answered.

Chapter Seventeen

Molly Means had the children huddled close to her. Lulu was snuggled in her arms. The tiny safe house she had built seemed to be doing the job. It felt like they had been trapped in this room for hours. In reality it was less than 40 minutes. Again Molly thought how fortunate it was for the kids that she was on duty tonight. Molly was in top shape and well prepared for the physical ordeal they now faced. She thought about the difficulties of carrying these children down a ladder. Molly was unaware the Local Fire Department was not responding. She had no idea that their only hope for survival was a group of old timers who had been drinking at a wedding. These guys were coming to get her but had fearsome obstacles to overcome.

The upper part of the ICU room was now full of smoke. Molly pulled the children closer. The kids were hanging on to their only hope for salvation. The children buried their faces in Molly's lap. Molly rested the arm that held Lulu on their heads.

When the back wall of the hospital crashed to the ground the kids started to cry. The noise and the jarring movement of the building frightened them. The children were calmer now but the high-pitched whistling sound was starting to unnerve Molly. It sounded like a giant teapot. God knows what was causing it. For sure it was not a good thing. Molly started to hum softly to comfort the children.

Joe set out our plan before we opened the door to the fifth floor hallway. The move down the corridor would be difficult because of the collapsed floor. We put on fresh tanks and assembled the gear we had carried up. Each of us would have an important task to perform.

The original explosion compromised the stability of the building. The force of the blast split the hallway floor right down the middle. It was hanging from the walls downward toward a gapping crack. It looked more like a ditch instead of a hallway. At certain points fire could be seen attempting to extend up from the corridor below.

Moving through this area was going to be extremely dangerous. We had to work as a team to get to the ICU room. I could see pain on Joe's face. The jump across the open stairwell must have injured his hip again. Joe didn't mention it but I knew he was hurting big time. We tied ourselves together like mountain climbers. If anyone slipped into the chasm the others would have a chance to pull him out.

Joe gave instructions. He said," Billy, you are going to lead us. Each wall has a support bar like the railings on a stairwell. We can use them to hang on to as we move forward. Try to support your weight on the floor as much as you can. I assume most areas will require hand over hand movement. As we move it is important the man behind you has secured himself to the wall. We are trying to save people here and don't want to get hung up trying to save each other."

"What shall I do when I get to the room sir?" Billy asked.

"Get inside and secure the rope to something solid. Remember this is the only rope we have and we need it to lower everyone down the outside wall."

The order of movement was the kid first, me next, and then Bolden. Joe would bring up the rear. Joe always took the most dangerous position. Our first task was to get the corridor door opened. It was jammed shut by the collapse of

126

the building. We let Billy take the first crack at it. We moved back to give him room to work.

Bolden told Billy, "Try to hit the hinges with your axe. If you break the door at those points we can push it in."

Billy started hacking the door with his axe.

It took only moments before the hinges were weakened enough to push the door in. Time was becoming an important factor in our quest. We could hear the blood-chilling howl of the superheated propane tanks. Those tanks scared the hell out of us but they were something we could not control. We had to stay focused on the problems we were facing in the corridor. We were depending on Danny and his crew to handle the tank problem. Our task was complicated enough so we kept our minds on getting to those kids as quickly as possible.

The door acted as a launching ramp. When it fell it covered the vee shape of the floor. It extended seven feet into the hallway. Joe instructed Billy to check every point where the railing attached to the wall. We had about a hundred feet of rope so Joe wanted to tie the excess rope to each securing point so there was a double safety factor in case we had to back out quickly.

Joe said, "Let's get this over with as quick as we can. Billy, move in and grab that railing. We are right behind you."

Billy moved forward on his hands and knees. He reached to his left and found the heavy wood railing. He got a firm grip with both hands like he was holding the rung of a ladder. Billy slowly moved off the door launching ramp and we were on the last perilous leg of our journey. There was too much smoke to see our destination. The crack in the floor was an eerie sight to behold. It looked like a jagged river leading us to hell. The light from the fire below gave the corridor a surreal glow and created enough visibility for us to see each other as we moved along the wall.

Billy put both feet on the slanting floor but supported most of his weight with his arms. He inched along to the area where the first rail connection was located. He took the excess line and secured it to this point. Billy moved on toward the next wall connector. As he moved the line tugged on the next man in line. The next man moved off the ramp and reached for the wall railing. Soon all four of us were moving toward the ICU room.

It was especially hard for us older guys. Supporting most of your weight with your arms is physically exhausting. It was like moving along a giant monkey bar with a hand over hand motion. There was a lot of slipping and sliding. The angle of the floor made it difficult to support your weight. It seemed you could move a few yards then your feet would slip causing you to hang from the railing. It was a struggle to pull yourself back up. You had to dig your toes into the slanted surface for support.

Billy was moving at a rapid pace. I had to shout to slow him down. The rope between us was pulled taunt as a hyper dog's leash. I was afraid he was going to pull me off the railing. The other guys paused momentarily to catch their breaths.

We were using up the air in our tanks at a rapid pace by working so hard. Everything was on a timer now. We didn't know what faced us in the ICU room. Was the fire into that area yet? Was the fire extending up the stairwell to cut us off? If we opened the door and found fire would we be trapped with no way out? It was a strange feeling hanging from that railing knowing that if we let go we would fall into the flaming crack. Sometimes it is better not to think. We were following Joe's orders like we had when we were on the Department. He always got us through.

Billy had done a good job of stringing the rope. If any part of the railing failed we would have a safety margin with the rope being tied to the anchor points. We would need every inch of the rope to reach our destination. If we made the room someone would have to go back and untie the rope from the wall connectors. The rope was needed to lower everyone down from the window. It is amazing how many problems have to be addressed at a fire. It is like building a house of cards. If you make one mistake everything is over.

Not much was said as we moved through the hallway. When we were strung out along the wall, Joe ordered us to stop. He went back and propped the door back into its frame. The door would prevent the fire from advancing for a few moments. Joe was buying us as much time as possible. We could hear that ungodly screeching and knew the fire was stalking us like a sinister predator. We were being chased by something that intended to kill us.

Moving down the hallway I thought how the incredible turn of events of the evening had brought us to this situation. An hour ago we were laughing, drinking, and dancing. We were now stretched out along the hall like men before the mast preparing to be flogged. The room was incredibly hot and the eerie glow of the fire made the corridor truly a scene from hell. I thought of our working days on the department. We would go from watching TV or playing ping pong to the most hellacious situations imaginable. Our response time, to a fire, was usually three minutes or less and the action was intense and immediate. Time was always a pressure point when working at a fire. This fire was no different. The only difference was how slow and out of shape we had become. Was this fire going the one that finally did us in? We would know that answer soon.

"How you doing Billy?" Joe shouted.

"Almost there sir. I can see the door."

"Get in as fast as you can and tie that line. We have to keep going. The fire is moving up the stairwell."

Molly heard the doorknob rattle. It was a welcome sound. She told the kids to stay put and slipped out of the safety enclosure. She crawled on hands and knees to the door. The smoke and heat in the room was tolerable but getting worse by the minute. She opened the door a crack and saw a familiar face. It was Billy Svenson. She reached out and grabbed Billy around the neck and helped him into the room.

"My god, Billy, am I glad to see you. Are you alone?"

"Hold on Molly. I got help with me. Help me tie this rope to something solid so we can get the guys with me into the room."

They found a pipe that ran from the floor to the ceiling and secured the safety line.

Billy returned to the doorway and helped us into the room. Joe told Billy to go back and detach the rope and bring it back into the room. Billy moved out into the corridor and started to move back along the wall. There was a whooshing sound and the heat level rose suddenly. Joe took a dive for the door and started to pull on the rope to get Billy back in the room. Billy was screaming for help. We jumped in to help Joe. We got our hands on Billy and jerked him over the thresh hold. Joe slammed the door. He couldn't get it shut. Hot tongues of flame were coming in through the small opening. The rope was stopping Joe from closing the door completely. With a crashing swing of his axe, Bolden cut the rope. It slipped into the hallway. Joe shut the door tightly and sealed the room from the attacking fire.

"This is the deal guys. The fire now owns the hallway. There is no going back. We have to find a way to get out of here through the window. We just lost our rope. Anyone have any ideas?" Joe asked.

Chapter Eighteen

Molly grabbed Billy's arm. She led him across the room to the makeshift shelter standing near the window. Billy followed Molly inside. The kids were crying. Molly gently hushed them and told them the Firemen were here. One of the older girls was holding Lulu. When Lulu spotted Billy she let out a squeal of delight. She lunged for her brother and was almost dropped by the girl holding her. Her little hands were extended toward Billy in an opening closing motion. Billy swept her into his arms. Tears were running down his cheeks. He nuzzled his precious little sister and cooed reassurances in her tiny soft ear.

He whispered, "Billy is here."

Billy knew the danger was not over but at least he had found his sister. He had confidence that Joe and his Firefighters would get them out somehow. The last few minutes were harrowing and filled with danger. The fire had literally chased us up the stairwell. It had followed us through the damaged corridor and was now beating on the ICU room door.

We reviewed our options. The only escape route was out the window. We couldn't use the corridor or stairwell. There was no communication link to the outside. We had lost the rope to the fire in the hallway. All we had were the few tools we managed to bring with us. There was an axe and a

Halligan bar that Joe and Bolden had carried with difficulty while climbing down the hallway railing. We needed those tools to bust the window out.

Experience told us our final moves had to be planned carefully. Joe knew exactly what we were going to do.

He explained, "We have to get the window open as soon as a ladder is raised. After the pane is broken out, I want the frame removed and all the glass cleared from the edges. Hopefully we can get the attention of those on the outside and they will get a ladder up to us. When we take the window out we must be prepared to move fast. The fire is looking for oxygen and will eat through the door to get it. Whatever kind of ladder they get up will not have a man on it. Bolden, I want you out first to secure the ladder. Bob you go next and take Lulu with you. The nurse goes second. Billy and I will be last." We will each carry kids as we move out.

We moved close to the window. We could barely see through the thick smoke outside. We could make out the rotating red and blue flashers of the rescue vehicles. When the wind momentarily cleared the smoke we could see the command post and Bobby working his two pumpers.

Joe told us to shine our flashlights out the window to attract attention. We aimed them at Bobby and tried to will him to look up. We were yelling and doing everything in our power to attract his attention. Bobby was concentrating on delivering water to the fire. Bobby knew Danny's crew was trying to cool the screeching propane tanks and were in extreme danger. If they lost water it would mean disaster. We realized he was doing his job but getting his attention was critical to solving our predicament.

Bobby was fine-tuning the pressure on the Seagrave. He was working four lines. The most important lines snaked across the parking lot and disappeared into the door of the building. These hoses were keeping his friends alive as they tried to hold back the fire and cool the propane tanks. The high-pitched screeching sound was starting to jangle everyone's nerves.

Bobby looked at the crowd. Most were farmers with a strong work ethic. They represented the best of America. They made wonderful volunteers and had done everything Bobby asked without question. They manned the hoses like pros. Together with the volunteers Bobby was doing a good job of holding the fire at bay. He knew the building was a total loss but they were not trying to save a structure. They were trying to save lives. Tonight we were just a group of old Firefighters doing our thing with every ounce of energy we possessed. Could we pull it off? Bobby knew the answer to that question would be answered shortly. Bobby had seen enough fires in thirty years to know the building would start collapsing soon. If the propane exploded it could happen sooner.

Bobby heard a murmur from the crowd as he moved around his rigs. He looked at their upturned faces. A few of them were pointing upward. He turned and looked.

Chapter Nineteen

Bobby kazoo's heart started to beat rapidly. He could see his friends at the window on the top floor of the burning building. The smoke was boiling up from the lower part of the hospital and at times obscured the location of the trapped Firefighters. They were waving and yelling frantically but Bobby could not hear them. The sound of the crowd, the roar of the accelerating blaze, and the thunderous throb of the pumping fire engines was drowning out everything but the wail of the super heated gas cylinders. The critical moment had arrived. From this point on there could be no mistakes. Every action would be a one time chance. Bobby knew he had to act fast to save his friends.

The heart of an attack on a blaze is the pumper and the pipe men who take the fight to the seat of the fire. The most important piece of equipment is the ladder truck. The truck crew will ventilate the building and make rescues as needed. Working as a team a pumper and a ladder truck are very effective in combating a fire. There was no ladder truck at this fire. Bobby would have to improvise.

Every ladder on the pumpers had been carried to the building and erected. Not one was long enough to reach the fifth floor. The longest one fell twenty feet short of the ICU room windowsill. It was a terrible dilemma.

During his years on the job Bobby didn't have to worry about the kind of fire problems he now faced. The Chief was responsible for the tough calls. Bobby became a Fire Engine Operator to avoid the stress and responsibility of making life and death decisions. Here he was now with the task of directing untrained volunteers to do things they were unfamiliar with under a pressure driven time frame. Bobby sank to a squatting position with his head down. He shut his eyes and tried to come up with answers.

When he opened his eyes he saw the men manning one of the hose lines had turned the stream into a window on the first floor where Danny and his guys were working. He had an instant vision of losing his fire engine at the train station fire many years ago when he was a rookie. The fire boat made a near fatal mistake of directing water into a building with men working inside. They were lucky no one died at that fire. Damn it my guys are going to get cut off Bobby thought. It was 50 yards from Bobby's location to the fire. Bobby knew he had to stop that line from rolling the fire back over the men in the hallway.

Bobby took off like a sprinter running the 100 yard dash. He came sliding up to the men manning the hose.

He screamed, "No, No, No."

He explained to the men what was happening. He told them to direct the water toward the top of the building. When he started to return to his rig he was gasping for air. He never felt so old. He ached all over and was not able to catch his breath. He still had to figure a way to help those trapped on the top floor. Bobby got a stabbing pain in the middle of his chest. He was sweating profusely and began to get dizzy. I have to slow up he thought. Bobby said a silent prayer and asked the lord to please keep him going for a little while longer.

Bobby's head started to clear as he reached his post in front of the gauges of the working pumper. He slowly lowered his body to sit on the running board of the old Seagrave. His legs were cramping and sweat dripped from his bowed head. He knew it was imperative that he get a ladder to those clinging to life on the fifth floor.

There were some teenagers standing near by and he motioned them over to where he was standing.

"Listen guys, we have a real problem here. Do any of you know where we can get a ladder long enough to reach that top floor?'

"No sir but we will try to find one."

They took off running toward the street. Bobby thought of every rescue incident he had witnessed during his time with the department. There had been cave ins, explosions, apartment building fires and odd ball deals like the workers trapped in the coal hopper. Bobby didn't want to think the worst but he remembered watching victims jump when the fire reached them on the upper floors of tall buildings. Getting his pals out of this building was going to be tough but Bobby was determined to pull it off. He racked his brain for a solution.

The only vision that came to mind was the harrowing rescue at the Buhl Building fire. At this incident a madman had entered the eighth floor office of an attorney who had allegedly bilked him out of some money. The assailant carried a can of gasoline and a twelve gauge shotgun.

He shot the receptionist the moment he entered the office. The blast caught her in the throat and decapitated her. She dropped like a sack of rocks and blood sprayed across the room. The people waiting in the room scattered like quail. The lucky ones made the hallway. The others ran into the inner office and slammed the door. A hail of gunfire followed them as the gunman empted his weapon. No one was hit and they moved desks and file cabinets against the door to keep the killer out.

The crazy man was screaming and pounding on the door. He finally got quiet and poured gasoline around the reception area. He splashed the walls and furniture with the accelerant. He reloaded his gun and stepped into the hallway. He pulled out a cigarette lighter and snapped the igniter to get a flame. He tossed the burning lighter into the room and closed the door. With a loud whoosh the office was instantly turned into a blazing inferno. Those trapped in the next room faced a horrible death.

Bobby remembered this incident because he was the driver of the first responding engine. When they arrived smoke was pouring out the eighth floor window. Several people were hanging out over the sill trying to get air. Their situation was desperate. If a rescue crew did not get to those people quickly there would be bodies crashing to the pavement in front of the Buhl Building.

Ladder One pulled directly under the window. With calm efficiency the hundred foot aerial ladder was raised toward the screaming victims. The end of the ladder stopped twenty feet short of the window. Time was a factor as angry black smoke began to envelope the people hanging out the window. Bobby remembered how Joe Barchilli and his squad performed an amazing rescue at this fire. Bobby grinned as he realized that the plan of rescue Joe devised so many years ago would be the method used to rescue him and the others from this fire in the hospital tonight.

Chapter Twenty

When the civilians directed water into the first floor window they created a dangerous situation for Danny and Barkley. They had fought their way down the long hall and around a corner. They were now at the end of another corridor and close to the sizzling propane tanks that were about to explode. They were directing water onto the howling containers. The fire behind them had snaked along the ceiling and managed to vent out a window. When the men outside hit the window with a hose stream it changed the dynamics of the fire. Both Firefighters sensed the change. The swirling movement of the smoke and a rise in temperature told them the fire was moving in another direction. If it was heading toward them they would have to abandon their present position and get out of the building quickly. It was a worrisome dilemma.

Barkley yelled. "Goddamn it Danny we can't go. Joe is depending on us. If these tanks blow they are dead."

"I know. I know. But we're dead too if the fire cuts us off. Why don't I stay here and you go back to check it out. Take your line with you. Maybe you can roll the fire back. I'll keep cooling these fricken tanks."

"You're right. It looks like our only option. I'm going back but if I yell for you to get out you have to promise you'll do it. Just drop your line and bail out. We can use my line to fight our way out."

"I promise. Now get your ass moving," Danny answered.

The sound of the screeching propane tanks made hearing difficult.

Barkley twisted the line and started to drag it back to the corner to stop the fire from moving behind them. Ordinarily it takes several Firefighters to move a charged line but with some effort a single man can do it. Barkley huffed and puffed as he dragged the line. He could feel the energy draining from his body. He was on his knees when he got to the corner. He looked up and saw the fire moving in a gentle undulating motion at the ceiling of the corridor. It had the appearance of a giant flat snake as it twisted and slithered along the top of the passageway. He knew it was deadlier than a snake.

Barkley rolled into a sitting position with his back against the wall. He was around the corner from Danny's corridor. From this point he could sweep his line up and down the hallway to hinder the fire. He was exhausted and drenched in sweat. He was wincing from the burns on his neck and ears. He turned his nozzle on the fire and hunkered down for the battle.

Slowly the fire started to roll back. Barkley now knew he could hold this position. He hoped the rescue team could accomplish their mission quickly. He did not know the ladder was too short to get the rescuers down. He did know his buddies would never abandon him, just like he would not abandon Danny.

He called down the hallway, "I think I can hold the fire back unless something changes. Remember if I start yelling, I want you to come out. You got that?"

"Okay, quit bitching at me," was the muffled reply.

Then it happened. The ceiling between Barkley and Danny collapsed with a roar. Debris and timbers came down and covered Barkley's right foot. The smoke that swirled around him was mixed with dust and sparks from the cave in. Barkley got up and shook the boards and plaster from his leg. He flashed his light on the jumble of debris that ran from the floor to the ceiling. It was packed almost solid. The only area open was a small portion of the hall near the floor. The hose that Danny was manning extended through this small opening and escaped being crushed. It was still supplying water to the other side of the cave in. It was a lucky break but Danny was trapped on the other side of tons of debris.

Barkley feared Danny had been buried in the collapse. He yelled to Danny," You okay?"

A muffled reply that was barely audible came back, "Yeah but were in a load of shit now. I got water but my tank gauge says I only have ten minutes of air left."

"Stay where you are and I will get help."

"Okay dumb ass. I'll stay here. Where do you think I'm going?"

Barkley shut down his line and scrambled back toward the doorway on his hands and knees. He had to stay low because the flames were rolling above him along the ceiling. He hated to leave Danny but he needed help to dig through the crap that now clogged the corridor. Danny was dead if they could not reach him before his air ran out. To make matters worse the propane tanks seemed to be getting louder. If they exploded there would be no need to make a rescue effort. Danny would be toast.

Danny sat with his back to the sealed off hallway. His heart was pounding and he was breathing hard. He was scared. Experience told him he had to calm down. His excitement was causing him to quickly use up the remaining air in his tank. He gathered his thoughts. Get as comfortable as you can and keep cooling the propane tanks. Keep your head and depend on Barkley. He knew his mates would get him out if there was any way possible. He got a knot in his gut when he thought it may not be possible. Do your best and stay positive was all he could think about.

Peering over the edge of the floor into the basement he could see several cheery red tanks. He was hitting the ones on top but there were others buried under a bed of hot coals. The water was not penetrating the coals and Danny knew it was only a matter of time before the heat ruptured those tanks. If he panicked he was dead. If he held his wits he was maybe dead later. He opted for the later choice.

Chapter Twenty One

Tobin Barkley stumbled out of the burning hospital. He saw several groups of people working the fire hoses. He looked at Bobby running his two pumpers. The scene was chaotic. Fire from the rear of the building lit the night sky. Smoke swirled around everything. At times the smoke obscured the men at the hoses. Barkley could see activity around one of the ladders. As he hustled toward Bobby he could see the rescue team was trapped at least twenty feet beyond the reach of the ladder.

Barkley gave Bobby a rundown of the problem they now faced.

"The hallway has collapsed and Danny is trapped. I need Joe and the guys to dig him out. We have to hurry because his air is going to run out."

"Joe is still in the building," Bobby replied. "We got a ladder up but it's too short. I got people looking for a longer ladder. I got an idea but it will be dangerous,"

"Talk to me. We don't have time to waste."

"Do you remember the Buhl Building fire?" Bobby asked.

"Yeah I do and it just might work."

Barkley was digging through the engine compartments when the teenagers returned with a long straight beam ladder.

One of the kids said, "We found this at the lumber yard mister. What do you want us to do with it?"

It was the first good break they had at this fire. Barkley found some leather belts in the compartment and ordered the teenagers to follow him. Flames were coming out the windows on the floor below the trapped victims. Barkley assembled the young men at the base of a ladder that had been erected against the wall of the building.

He explained the plan," What we are about to attempt is risky but it is the only option we have. I want you two big guys to steady the base of this ground ladder. I want you other two guys to carry this straight beam ladder up to the top of the ground ladder and set it on the second or third rung from the top and raise it to where you see those people at the window. Make sure you secure it with these leather belts. Do you understand?"

There was a moment of dumbfounded silence.

"Holy shit mister. Do you think this will work?" One of the boys asked.

"Yes. I was part of a team that made a rescue at the Buhl Building. We got six people out of the eighth story of an office building under similar circumstances. It wasn't easy but we pulled it off. We can do the same thing here," Barkley explained.

The kids agreed to do it. Barkley looped the leather belts around the first guy's shoulders and helped him start up the ladder. They had to move slowly climbing one step at a time because they were carrying the straight beam ladder. Smoke enveloped the teenagers as they began their assent. Their eyes were burning and they coughed from the swirling smoke. Barkley yelled to the men manning the hoses. He ordered them to keep the flames away from the ladder. He told the kids holding the ladder they were on their own. He had to return to the fire to get Danny out.

Barkley headed back to the hallway. He figured he had been gone about five minutes. He saw a pile of tools and extra air bottles piled near the entrance of the building. Bobby must have had them placed there. Bobby was one great engineer he thought. He was thinking all the time. Thank god he was here tonight. Barkley knew he needed help to dig Danny out. The immediate problem was to get an air bottle to his buddy so he wouldn't suffocate. He remembered the small opening near the floor left by the collapsed ceiling. He hoped he could pass a tank through that small passageway. He feared the opening might not be big enough. It was a desperate situation but this whole fucking fire was a desperate situation.

Barkley knelt down at the entrance to the hall. He reached for his face piece and strapped it to his face. He pulled the tabs tight to create a good seal. He checked his regulator and saw he had only minutes of air left before his warning bell went off. No time to change this bottle I got to get a tank to Danny he thought.

He picked up a pike pole from the stacked tools. He grabbed two air bottles and struggled into the doorway with his unwieldy load. Ugly flames were venting at the top of the door as the fire started to claim the hallway. Barkley had to stay low to avoid the extreme heat. He had to move in a long way to make the corner where he left the hose nozzle. He stumbled and fell against the wall but kept going. It was impossible to see so he maintained contact with the wall so he would not blunder past the turn where Danny was trapped.

At the corner he paused and used the line to stop the advancing fire. He rolled it back again toward the rear of the building. He then proceeded to where the collapse had occurred.

He called to Danny, "I'm back partner. How're you doing?"

He could hear the warning bell on Danny's breathing apparatus indicating he only had a few minutes of air left.

A muffled answer came back, "I'm doing Ok for a dying man. You got any air for me?"

At that moment Barkley's warning bell started to ring. He knew he had to move fast.

He yelled to Danny, "I'm going to push an air bottle to you under this collapse. There's an opening where the wall and floor connect. Do you see it?"

"Yeah I see it. I'm guessing we got about six or eight feet between us. Can you slide a bottle through this mess?"

"I think so. I got a pike pole to help me push it through."

Barkley got down on the floor and slid the aluminum tank into the hole. It was a tight fit. The air bottle was approximately ten inches in diameter. He put the top in first hoping the debris would not damage the threads on the connecting valve. He slid it in as far as he could. So far so good he thought. Next he took the pike pole and pushed it into the opening like a gunner loading an old war cannon. Barkley heard the scraping sound as the tank moved through an ever narrowing space. He could hear Danny's warning bell mixed with the screech of the hot propane tanks.

Danny yelled, "It's coming. I can feel it."

The bottle almost made it before it hung up. Barkley pushed as hard as he could but it would not move further. There were only a few more inches to go but the tank was hopelessly wedged between the wall and the collapsed debris. The only thing protruding was the valve and the threads at the top of the tank.

Barkley had to stop. His air had run out and his mask was constricting on his face as he sucked for air. He rolled over and desperately looked for the other air bottle. He found it and sat up to remove his harness. Ordinarily a Firefighter could keep his harness on while another man changed the bottle. To do it alone required taking the apparatus off. His hands were shaking as he fumbled with the threads on the regulator. He soon had the tank in operating order and slid the apparatus onto his back and secured the belt and shoulder straps. He turned the handle on the tank and was again breathing from a fresh air supply.

Danny was involved in a terrible situation on the other side of the collapse. He couldn't get the air bottle all the way through the opening. He too had run out of air. Dropping his harness he detached the spent bottle. He laid the apparatus as close to the wedged tank as possible. Luckily Barkley had pushed the tank through with the valve side first. Danny could reach the threads of the bottle with his regulator hose. Lying on his stomach he reached in and made the hook up. The entire assembly was now on the floor with the shattered plaster and ashes. Danny didn't care. He slipped on his face piece and felt the cool soothing air fill his lungs. He sat with his back against the collapsed debris. As long as he didn't have to move he could use the air tank. It didn't matter, he wasn't going anywhere until they dug him out anyway.

Chapter Twenty Two

The fire was almost in complete control of the building. It had trapped Danny behind the collapsed ceiling. The flames were trying to bypass Tobin Barkley's position and he was in danger of being cut off from escape. The rescue team was huddled in the intensive care room with only one way out. If they didn't get a ladder up to their position soon they were goners. The fire had followed our team up the stairwell and down the fifth floor corridor like a stalking animal. Flames now roared and chewed at the safety glass separating the ICU room from the hall. It was only a matter of time until the heat of the inferno would break the glass and kill the occupants of the room.

Joe knew Bobby had spotted them waving from behind the window. Bobby raised his arm with an index finger and pointed at Joe. That gesture said that help was on the way. The spotlights from the rigs were turned toward the fifth floor window. Like a stage play the final act was about to begin.

Joe said, "Get ready everyone. I can see some people bringing another ladder."

All eyes were on the young men proceeding upwards. Their movements were slow and deliberate. They were straining to carry the heavy straight beam ladder and clung ever closer to the ladder they were climbing as they ascended. They were frightened but knew they must keep going. These guys had never done anything like this but were making a valiant effort to pull it off.

Joe told everyone to stand back. He took a swing with his axe and shattered the window. The shards of glass exploded outward. They fell like snow barely missing the young men coming up the ladder. The accumulated smoke in the room rushed out and cool air rushed in with a promise of escape.

The kids were frightened by the smashing of the glass. They were screaming and crying. The place was a madhouse of noise. The yowling of the kids blended with the sound of the super heated propane tanks. The din added fear to the room. We were glad to be leaving this hell hole even if we had to risk our lives going down the rickety ladder.

The guys bringing up the ladder finally made it. The kid at the top stopped and half turned his body. He began to feed the splice ladder upward. It seemed like it took forever to reach the fifth floor windowsill.

Joe took off his belt and told us to do the same. We took the belts and fashioned a securing line that Joe attached to the top of the ladder. He wrapped it around a water pipe on the sink near the window. It was flimsy as hell but it was all we had.

Bolden was leaning out the window watching the guy make the final ties securing the top ladder to the rungs of the ground ladder. When the kid was done he looked up and waved. Bolden shouted for the two guys to go down and made an up down gesture with his hand. They were half way down when Bolden swung his body outward and over the sill. He reached tentatively with his foot until he found the top rung of the ladder. It took only seconds and he disappeared from sight as he went down to check the securing belts. Once the bindings were checked Bolden positioned himself behind the splice ladder with his back toward the building. He set his feet one rung up on the ground ladder and placed his hands on the outer rails of the top spliced ladder. He would serve as an anchor to keep the top ladder steady.

He yelled, "Come on Joe get your asses moving. Those god damn tanks are going to blow any minute now."

Bolden was right about those tanks. If they blew we were done for. Time was of the essence and we moved toward the window. The hoses below us threw water into the windows on each side of the ladder. Everything was getting wet and slippery from the over spray. The smoke was thick and at times we could not see the ground. The safety glass on the window separating us from the hallway was starting to crack from the extreme heat of the fire. If the window failed we would be incinerated by the advancing fire. We had to move fast.

Joe grabbed my shoulder and said, "Get moving Bob."

I swung my body out onto the ladder. I looked down and immediately wished I hadn't. The flimsiness of the set up was appalling. It was like standing on a stack of fiddle sticks. My heart was pounding in my chest as I turned to look back into the intensive care room. What I saw scared me even more. The people in the room were looking outward and didn't see the angry mass of orange and red fire trying to bust through that last bit of safety glass. I yelled for Joe to hand me some of the kids.

Out came Lulu. She was screaming the instant she was separated from Billy. I got a good grip on her and reached for the next kid. My right arm was long enough to go around both of them. They didn't understand the danger they were in. They squirmed and pushed against my chest. I wanted to get down as quick as possible. It was spooky as hell but I made it down the steep splice ladder. I smiled as I passed Bolden. He was holding the two ladders together and he smiled back at me. We knew we were nearing the end of a difficult rescue. I moved at a more assured pace down the ground ladder. As I neared the ground I could feel arms and hands reaching to help me. Before I was all the way down, one of the men took the bigger child from my arms. I still had Lulu and was determined to keep her until Billy came down.

Next out was Molly Means. Joe handed her the biggest kid. The youngster was about seven years old and must have weighed sixty pounds or so. Joe told the kid to keep his arms and legs wrapped around Molly. The wind was blowing and Molly's skirt was flying in all directions. She steadied herself as the child gripped her neck with his hands clenching her hair in a death grip. Down she came. She whispered thank you when she passed by Bolden. The men on the ground helped her as she neared the ground. There was a lot of cheering and clapping as we brought those kids down but we were not out of danger yet.

I prayed the safety glass would hold long enough for the rest of them to get out. I looked toward Bobby standing by the fire engines. He was frantically waving at me to come over to him. I felt like a beaten dog as I slowly started to jog over to where he was working. There were several volunteers moving with me. One of them pointed out Lulu's mother. She was running toward us.

Lulu saw her too and turned with out stretched arms. I handed the baby over as we met. Lulu and her mom melded into one as they hugged and cried. The distraught women whispered reassurances into the baby's curly blond hair. I kept moving and heard the lady call after me with words of thanks. It made me feel good. I was exhausted and hurt all over. I felt a sense of pride knowing my old Firefighter pals had made a pretty good rescue at this fire.

Bobby was holding a fresh air bottle when I got to him.

"God I'm glad to see you," he said.

He spun me around and detached the nearly spent tank on my back. He explained the situation as he finished tightening the threads on the fresh air bottle. He turned me around and I saw apprehension in his eyes.

He said, "A collapse has blocked the hallway. Danny is trapped. Barkley is in there alone trying to dig him out. You have to get in there to help them. Be sure to take extra tanks."

I stood dumbfounded for only a second then turned to go back into the fire. I looked at the whole crazy scene as I crossed the parking lot. The hospital was a total loss. It looked like it had been bombed. The rear of the structure had collapsed and angry red fire boiled skyward mixed with seething black smoke. I could see fire in every window on the fifth floor except where the ICU room was. I knew anyone left had to get out of there quickly. I followed the hose lines back toward the hallway.

Chapter Twenty Three

At the entrance I paused to put my mask on. I pulled the tabs tight and put on the helmet Bobby had handed me. I picked up a shovel and extra air bottles as I moved into the building. It was hot and smoky. I yelled for Barkley and he yelled back letting me know where he was. I could hear his hose open full bore beating the fire back.

He was in a kneeling position when I got to him. I knelt beside him and put my face piece close to his so we could hear each other. He told me Danny was behind a pile of plaster and timbers a short distance down the corridor.

He said, "Take the line and hold this position while I try to dig him out. We ain't got much time."

I let him know that help was on the way. Joe was bringing the last kid down as I was coming into the building. Once they were down they could help free Danny. He disappeared into the smoke and moments later I could hear him hacking away at the debris pile.

The fire around the propane tanks was getting hotter. Danny directed his hose stream onto the roaring mess but it was a losing battle. He was sucking air at a prodigious rate. His mouth was dry and his heart was pounding. He was running on pure adrenaline. His thoughts were racing. He was trapped like a rat and prayed his buddies could somehow get him out of there. The reality of the situation told him that escape was a long shot. He knew what was likely to happen. He had seen propane explode before. There is a blinding flash followed by a murderous shock wave that crushes everything in its path. The heat comes next. It fries anything left to a crisp. His eyes filled with tears as he thought of his wife and children. He would miss watching his grand kids grow up.

Danny turned and yelled to Barkley," Tobin get your ass out of here. No use both of us dying. I'm through as soon as my air runs out anyway."

"Screw you Danny. I'm staying until I get you out of there. Joe and Bolden are on the way and we'll get this crap moved."

"Bullshit. The rest of this ceiling is ready to come down. This building is toast. If these tanks blow you guys will get buried for sure."

Tears started to stream down Barkley's cheeks. He knew what Danny said was true. He promised himself to stay until Joe got there. He would let Joe make the decision.

Outside the rescue was going smoothly. Billy climbed onto the ladder and Joe handed him two of the crying kids. Billy started down. He knew safety was waiting at the bottom of the ladder. His main concern was his sister Lulu and she was now safe on the ground. He was amazed at the courage of these old Firefighters. They helped him rescue his sister. He looked up as he passed Bolden. He could see Joe getting on the Ladder with the last little kid. Moments later Billy was on the ground. He looked up again.

Suddenly there was a whooshing sound and the sky lit up. The safety glass had finally failed. The fire charged into the intensive care room like an angry linebacker looking for a quarterback. It came roaring out the window inches above Joe's head. The force of the blast shook the flimsy ladder and Joe heard the securing belts pop as they gave way. Joe's helmet was blown off and shot in an arc all the way to Bobby Kazoo's rig. It ricocheted off the back of the fire engine with a thud and spun wildly on the ground like a spinning plate. It startled Bobby and he looked up at a horrifying sight.

The ladder slid to the left about two feet. Joe's weight was pulling the ladder down. He had to move fast to get off the ladder or crash to the pavement below. Bolden was straining to hold the weird contraption of ladders together. He yelled for Joe to hurry.

What Joe did next made everyone watching gasp in disbelief. He took a short step backward and free fell down the ladder. As his feet came off the rungs he spread his legs and caught the insoles of his boots on the outer rails of the ladder. His hands were on the outer rails and acted as a sliding guide as he fell. It was like sliding the pole at the fire house. Joe dropped half way down to where Bolden was trying to hold the ladders together. He began applying the brakes. He put as much pressure as he could on his insoles and squeezed hard with his hands. The over spray from the hoses made the ladder super slippery. Joe's bad hip made his right leg weak so he only had three contact points that were effective. If he could not stop his momentum before he came to the junction of the ladders he would crash into the ground ladder and fall to the ground. The little kid he was carrying was facing Joe and had a death grip around his neck. His little legs were wrapped around Joe's pot belly. He was screaming with fear. It was a muffled sound because his face was buried in Joe's chest. Joe gritted his teeth as he tightened his grip. He could feel the heat from friction through his gloves as he tried to stop the acceleration.

Bolden was looking up and saw Joe coming. He removed his hands from the outer rails. He braced his feet on the rungs of the ground ladder and leaned backward into the building. He knew he could not stop Joe's decent and didn't want to be knocked off the ladder if Joe hit the junction point too hard.

Joe realized he was not going to be able to stop his momentum. The ladder he was on was falling to the left in a deadly arc. One of the connecting belts on the rung where Bolden had planted his feet snapped with a cracking twang.

When Joe hit the junction of the two ladders he was still going too fast to stop. He released his feet from the rails of the upper ladder and tried to hit the top rung of the ground ladder which sat at an outward angle. The splice ladder he just came off of continued in its deadly arc and Joe saw it go past him as it fell four stories to the ground. The remaining connecting strap jerked the ground ladder before it snapped free. The men on the ground struggled to keep the ladder in an upright position. The weight of the two Firefighters at the top created an over balance and the laws of physics started a lever action that was difficult to overcome. Those on the ground lunged with out stretched arms to stop the ladder from falling. Slowly they regained control. At the top of the ladder was an amazing sight. Joe missed the rung with his feet. They had passed through the opening between the rungs. The impact on his thigh snapped the bone like a dry twig. He hung upside down like a trapeze artist. The sudden stop flipped Joe and tore the kid from his body. Joe grabbed for the child as he bounced free and barely managed to grasp his arm. Everyone held their breath as the situation stabilized. Fire was venting out the window where moments before we had been standing in the room. Bolden was balancing himself on the top rung of the remaining ladder with his back to the wall. He had nothing to hold on to. His arms were outstretched in a spread eagle manner. His fingers clawed at the wall as he struggled to maintain his balance. He looked like a high diver ready to plunge off a tower. He looked down carefully trying not to move his head. He could see Joe and the kid dangling below him.

Joe knew his leg was broken but he had a firm grip on the ladder rung with his other leg. He heard Billy shout that he was coming up to help him. Billy was fast as a cat. He was up in an instant and managed to get a grip on the child dangling from Joe's outstretched arm.

"Hang on Joe I will be right back," Billy said as he descended to the ground.

"Thanks kid but hurry up. I'm tired of hanging around this place."

Billy was half way down before he realized that Joe had made a joke of his situation. What wonderful men these guys were he thought. He dropped the child into the reaching arms of those below him and started back to help Joe.

Joe had righted himself by the time Billy got back.

"Go by me Billy and see if you can help Bolden."

Billy moved around Joe who was coming down one rung at a time on his remaining good leg. Billy moved near Bolden who was still in a high dive position at the top of the ladder. It was impossible for Bolden to bend forward without falling. He would have to depend on Billy to get him down safely.

"Okay kid, listen to me carefully. Move up as high as you can and put your head and shoulders against my legs like you are tackling me. Make sure you lock your legs into the rungs of the ladder like a trapeze catch man. When we are ready I am going to move forward and drop down. It's important you keep me pinned to the wall. You got that?" Bolden instructed.

"Yes sir I'm ready."

It was an act of faith for Bolden to step forward in a free fall. He trusted Billy. The kid had proven himself on the dangerous trip up the stairwell and down the smoke filled corridor.

Billy grunted and strained as Bolden slid down the wall. When he was down far enough, Bolden gripped the ladder with his hands. He told Billy to start down. Soon both were on the ground. They could hear the crowd yelling and cheering. Bolden grabbed Billy and kissed his soot stained cheek.

"Thanks kid. You got guts," he whispered in his ear.

"Thank you for getting my sister out," Billy shouted as he sprinted to where his mom was holding Lulu and smiling.

Chapter Twenty Four

Bolden looked toward Bobby who was pointing emphatically at the door of the building where the rest of the guys were fighting the fire. He was not aware that Danny was trapped. Bobby's body language told him that it was important for him to get inside to help out. The EMS placed a stretcher at the foot of the ladder and gently eased Joe unto the gurney. A doctor needed to look at his broken leg. Bolden took Joe's hand and told him he would see him at the hospital.

Bolden had left his tank and harness in the intensive care room. He moved to the fire engine where Bobby had a fresh air pac waiting for him. Bolden turned his back and Bobby helped him don the apparatus. They talked as they worked.

"You guys put on quite an act when you came out that window."

"Yeah, I thought I was going to end it with a swan dive."

Bobby explained the predicament confronting them inside the fire. He described the collapse and the efforts being made to dig Danny out. It was a tough deal because the tanks were unpredictable and could explode at any moment. Bolden nodded and started for the building. He was putting on his mask as he ran. At the entrance he stopped and turned on his air tank. He bent over and picked up a large pry bar and two extra tanks. Bobby saw him disappear into the smoke filled doorway. This would be the final action at this fire. It would be the hardest most physical job of the night.

When a collapse occurs the debris is usually a mixture of plaster, burning embers, and building materials like wood and steel. All this crap will congeal into a semi solid mass that is difficult to penetrate. When you add smoke, fire, and heat to the picture it becomes an awesome task to dig through it.

Bolden followed the sound of the crashing water and was soon at the junction of the halls. He reached down and patted me on the shoulder as he moved by. He kept going guided by the sound of Barkley's axe whacking the debris pile. He had to be careful as he moved forward so he would not be hit by the back swing of the axe. He yelled to let Barkley know help had arrived.

Barkley stopped swinging his axe and told Bolden that he was having difficulty penetrating the collapse.

"I can hardly dent this crap. Got any ideas?"

"No. Are you sure he is still alive?" Bolden asked.

"Hey, are you still in there?" shouted Barkley.

"I told you to get the hell out of here. Are you stupid or something? Do it now or we'll both ride the same bus to hell. Get going god damn it. I mean it, Barkley," Danny answered.

"I got help. Bolden is here."

"Good, that means they got out of the building. Did they get the kids out?"

"Yeah and now were going to get you out," Barkley answered.

"No you are not. I only have five minutes of air left. You can hear these propane tanks getting louder and I'm sure they're ready to blow."

"Bolden chipped into the conversation, "Danny you wouldn't leave us so why do you think we will leave you?"

Danny's voice started to break, "Bolden you're a good man and I know you're not stupid. We've been to a lot of fires together. I'm a dead man and I don't want to take you guys with me. You both know this is an impossible deal here. Now get going while you still have time."

Bolden and Barkley stood close to each other. Their eyes met as they looked through the plexi-glass of their masks. Barkley slowly shook his head. Bolden dropped his eyes and nodded his head in assent. They knew Danny was right.

Barkley whispered hoarsely, "I been here five minutes and I ain't moved shit. We got to try something else. Come on. Let's see if we can get above the collapse. If we make the next floor up we can drop in from above. "

Bolden agreed and yelled their plan to Danny, "Hang on buddy we're going to try to get you from the second floor."

"Get your asses moving," Danny answered.

The Firefighters turned and headed out. They were running low and stumbled into me at the corner of the hall. They fell in a heap. They scrambled to their feet, grabbed my arm, and jerked me toward the exit. We just cleared the hallway when the explosion occurred.

Chapter Twenty Five

It was over fast for Danny. The tanks had been simmering in a bed of hot coals. There were actually four tanks but only two were exposed. Danny was cooling the top two tanks but those underneath slowly got hotter and hotter. The temperature heated the compressed gas to a point where the expansion pressure was stronger than the steel that contained it. The first tank let out a scream and exploded.

Danny heard a sudden escalation in pitch just before the shock wave slammed into him. The force of the blast caught him full in the chest. It was like being hit by a speeding locomotive. The power of the expanding gas molecules was unstoppable. The white-hot fire that followed disintegrated Danny's body. His soul stepped into Firefighter's Valhalla in a blaze of glory.

The hallway we just vacated became a giant cannon barrel. The force of the explosion propelled the debris outward like a bullet shot from a gun. There was a grinding rushing noise that sounded like an avalanche. Several tons of debris hurtled down the corridor and slammed into the wall behind us. We were lucky. We missed being crushed by only a few steps. The impact drove the wall outward a few feet and the whole rear of the building came crashing down. A mass of wood splinters and dust washed over us. We were knocked to the floor. The sound of the blast left a ringing pain in our ears. Barkley was last in line and took most of the shock wave in his back. He was knocked unconscious. Bolden was on his knees trying to put his mask on. I grabbed him and told him to help me drag Barkley out of there. The rest of the building was ready to come down. We took Barkley's arms and dragged him toward the exit.

Out side Bobby Kazoo was stunned. He was watching the fire grow in intensity when the propane exploded. The first tank started a chain reaction. The second tank blew up a split second after the first. An enormous fireball propelled the other two tanks several hundred feet into the air. They exploded into spectacular fireballs. Our lives were saved by the compacted debris that caused Danny's death. It prevented the fire from moving down the hallway like a blowtorch to incinerate us. We had to hurry. The blast destroyed our hoses and the fire would quickly reclaim the hallway we were using to get out of the building.

The doomed building was creaking and grinding as it settled after the explosion. The ceiling in the hall was beginning to sag. We had about twenty feet to go. The cracking sounds got louder and I was afraid we were going to be buried in another collapse.

What happened next was a lucky break. It was a weird occurrence. It was a twist of fate that saved our lives. There was a big water tank on the roof of the hospital that stood on four legs. It had the words Cheboygan Community Hospital printed on its side and was a landmark you could see for miles when approaching the city.

The blast and subsequent collapse tilted the tank which held tons of water. Bobby Kazoo watched in amazement as the hospital started to disintegrate. The water tank tilted and in slow motion began to tumble downward. Just before the tank hit the roof it started to spill water. With a swooshing sound the water met the swirling flames. The huge volume of water punched a hole in the fire and gushed into the hallway where we had been fighting the fire. A tidal wave of water rushed down the corridor past the area where we tried to dig Danny out. It slammed into the wall and turned toward us. In an instant we were submerged in a cauldron of wood lath, mud and water. The three of us were picked up by the deluge and hurtled through the doorway to safety.

Bobby ran toward us. Fire apparatus began to arrive on the scene. The rigs had returned from the University and Firefighters were dismounting ready for action. Everyone was running to help the men who had been miraculously ejected from the building like a spent cartridge from a rifle. We were in a sitting position soaked to the bone. Barkley regained consciousness and sat with his back to me and Bolden.

Barkley spoke first, "What the hell just happened?

"We just saved your ass," Bolden answered.

I started to laugh. Only seconds ago I thought we were dead men and now we were sitting in a heap in the middle of the parking lot. It felt good to be alive. Bobby and the Firefighters got to us at the same time.

Bobby asked, "Where's Danny?"

We looked down with our eyes. We didn't have to tell him. He knew the answer.

Chapter Twenty Six

It was a crisp November morning. A crowd assembled in the parking lot of Holy Redeemer Church. The sky was filled with long lumpy gray clouds that scudded eastward like huge dirigibles. The sun peeked through occasionally to observe the spectacle that was taking place in back of the old church. It was football weather. It reminded me of the days when Danny and I played high school ball for the Southwestern Prospectors. He had been a hell of a running back. He was tough as nails and loved to mix it up. Those memories put a lump in my throat and my eyes misted with tears. Our high school and Holy Redeemer Church were about a mile apart. They were located in the heart of the Seventh Battalion where Danny and I had been Firefighters for most of our working lives.

Bolden, Barkley, Borza and I stood on one side of the entrance that led to the church altar. Facing us were Bobby Kazoo, Mac Pierce, Lee Long and Billy Svenson. We were Danny's pallbearers and we glistened and shined in our dark navy blue uniforms. The City of Detroit had given us permission to wear our uniforms for the funeral. The chevrons and patches we wore told a story. Our medals spoke silently of what we had done. The kid, Billy Svenson, wore a new suit. His blond hair was neatly combed and sparkled like gold when the sun hit it. Standing in the doorway was Joe. His leg was in a hip high plaster cast. He stood tall and straight on his crutches. Joe would not be able to carry the casket but would lead us into the church. The sun that highlighted the kid's hair reflected off the chest full of medals on Joe's uniform. Each medal had been earned at a price. Many represented the saving of a life. Joe was a Fireman's Fireman. He was our hero.

I could see the tears in Joe's eyes as the hearse turned into the church courtyard. This was going to be a tough day for all of us. The morning sun added a tinge of red to the clouds. It seemed Mother Nature was adding a touch of appropriate color to this solemn affair. We could hear the low throaty rumble of the diesel engines of the fire apparatus as they moved into position in front of the church.

Danny would be carried to the cemetery on the hose bed of Engine 27. We pall bearers would ride the side and rear of the rig as it took Danny on his last run. Two bag pipers moved to the front steps of the church and waited for the ceremony to begin. They were impressive to look at. They wore traditional tartans and tall bear skin hats. Positioned on both sides of the entrance and on every other step to the street was the Fire Department Honor Guard. They wore chrome military helmets and carried M-1 rifles.

The crowd was huge. Junction Avenue was closed from Vernor Highway to the expressway. Engine 27 pulled in front of the church next to the curb. Directly behind the rig was a limo carrying Danny's family. In line following were fire engines from many departments. There was the old Arhens Fox and a host of chief's cars. The media was present and I could see the mayor's limousine pulling into the parking lot.

Most of the department's off duty Firefighters were in attendance. Chief of Department Jimmy Walker had them lined up in ranks stretching down the street toward Engine 27s quarters. The men were all spit and polish. They wore white gloves and every badge had a piece of black tape across it to signify the loss of a brother Firefighter. The mayor stepped from his limo and started past the men, I heard Chief Walker shout, "Aaaa-ten...shun."

As one the ranks of Firefighters snapped to attention and held that posture until the mayor passed by. The Chief gave the order to stand at ease.

Four police motorcycles pulled to the front of the procession. They sat waiting with blue and white lights flashing. Riding the two front bikes were officers Jim Kelly and Mel Dupree. They were the men who were trapped as they risked their lives to save victims of the fire. It was good to see them again. The red lights and dome flashers on the fire department rigs were slowly rotating. A news helicopter flew overhead to record the somber proceedings. It would be a grand funeral for one of the cities bravest.

The hearse pulled close and stopped. The funeral director motioned for the pallbearers to come forward to take Danny into the church. We stood on both sides of the vehicle at the rear door. The coffin was moved on rollers so we could reach the side handles. The coffin was beautiful. The Firemen's Fund had commissioned an artist to create something special for Danny. The Fund is an organization that takes care of the widows and orphans of Firefighters lost in the line of duty.

The sarcophagus was spectacular. It was made of hand polished oak. The carrying handles were six foot pike poles made of a darker wood with gleaming brass tips. The lid was a mix of artwork and carvings fashioned from brass and chrome. The artist had sculpted hydrants, axes, helmets and replicas of the tools of our trade. They flowed across the coffin in an eye-pleasing pattern. At the center of the artwork was a Maltese cross with Danny's name inscribed in a beautiful script with artful curls and graceful lines to the letters.

The choir was singing Ave Maria and all stood as we carried Danny into the church. The priest and altar boys were waiting. We placed Danny before the congregation close to the altar and the ceremony began. There was complete silence in the church except for the soft sounds of people sobbing or the occasional muffled cough. Danny's wife and two daughters were holding up well. One of the girls gave a short heart rending eulogy about what a special dad Danny had been. When she finished it was my turn. I took a deep breath and stepped to the podium.

I believed I was able to lighten the mood when I talked about Danny's life. I told the assembly how Danny and I ran the streets of southwest Detroit as kids. Hell when we were 16 we thought we owned those streets. We eventually became Firefighters dedicated to protecting those streets and the people who lived there. I wanted everyone to know that Danny had not been afraid to die. In those last moments in the burning corridor, Danny was more concerned about saving those kids and getting his buddies out of the building than he was for his own well being. He gave his life willingly and with purpose. In the words of scripture," One has no greater love than to give one's life so his brother may live."

As we carried the coffin out of the church the choir sang the beautiful Irish ballad, Danny Boy. There was not a dry eye in the place. The last words I heard as we passed through the doorway were, "Danny boy I love you so."

We passed the honor guard on the steps. They stood at attention straight and tall. Their weapons were held at present arms. Their commander snapped his arm in a traditional military salute. The bag pipers were playing a low dirge as we descended the steps. Three Tomcat fighter planes came screaming in over Junction Avenue. When they passed over the church one of them separated and left the formation. The sun popped out of the clouds and sent soft warm rays of light over Danny's coffin. We raised the sarcophagus to waiting hands to be placed on the hose bed of Engine 27. The Firefighters covered it with a flag and secured it with bindings. We were ready to go. The motorcycles revved their motors as the procession started down the street. We would be leaving the Seventh battalion to go to the cemetery but first we would do a drive by of Engine 27s quarters.

Engine 27, Ladder 8 and Chief 7 all shared the same fire house. Ladder 8 had been moved to the platform in front of the fire hall. Every apparatus in the Battalion was lined up at the curb. There were four pumpers and a ladder truck. The lights and flashers on the apparatus were blinking a silent farewell to Danny. The men were lined up next to their rigs. Everyone wore pressed working blues and boots. Each company saluted as we passed by. When Engine 27 was directly in front of the engine house you could hear the bell on Ladder 8 ringing a tribute to a lost running mate. The men of Ladder 8 saluted and at the end of their formation stood a pair of empty boots. It was a reminder of how we can be lost but never forgotten.

Chapter Twenty Seven

The procession moved faster after we passed by Danny's company quarters. Firefighters from across the country were in attendance. There were fire engines from the suburbs and numerous chief's cars. The procession stretched out for over a mile.

We went through downtown Detroit on the way to the cemetery. A huge bronze arm hangs suspended, as a tribute to Joe Louis, in front of city hall. Thoughtful city workers placed a black arm band around the bicep of the statue. Office workers and pedestrians lined the curbs. They removed their hats and bowed their heads as the procession passed by.

We soon arrived at the cemetery gates. Danny was to be buried in the special section reserved for Firefighters. His plot was located on a hill facing the Detroit River. Across the river was Belle Isle. Looking across the river you could see an open area near the shore of the island. This is where Firefighters from Engine 32 said they would sometimes see the ghosts of the fire horses. At the highest point of the hill, near Danny's burial site, was the Firemen's Memorial Statue. It depicts a turn of the century Firefighter. He is a muscular man with a bushy mustache. In one hand he carries an axe and in his other arm is a little girl he just rescued. The inscription at the base pays homage to those who go in harms way to serve the people of the city. Surrounding the statue are rows of white crosses and gravestones. Some of the markers have dates reaching back to the late eighteen hundreds. I recognized the names on some of the newer ones. This is hallowed ground for Detroit Firefighters.

The sky became overcast and the clouds darkened. A cold wind blew in from the river as we stopped the rig at the foot of the memorial statue. There were hundreds of Firefighters standing in ranks facing the burial site. Chairs were set up for the family and I could see Danny's wife and daughters sitting there holding hands. The ground leading to the site was covered with flowers and wreathes. The Department Chaplain and Chief Walker stood waiting for the casket to be brought forward so the final ceremonies could begin.

I looked up at the statue of the old time Firefighter. In my mind I pictured Jack Montgomery and the fire horses going on a run. I thought about how many times men like Danny and Jack risked their lives for others. Those who serve in the fire service have a spirit that transcends the soul. I could feel the presence of that spirit as we dismounted to carry Danny to his final resting place.

A strange thing happened as we took the coffin off the rig. The sky grew even darker and a strong wind began to shake and bend the trees. With a rush of sound the wind twisted over the spot we stood and spiraled upward like a mini cyclone. Leaves and debris soared skyward as if the hand of God reached down to take Danny's soul to heaven. As quickly as it started the wind died down. There was silence and the warming rays of the sun burst through the clouds and stayed until the services were over.

The luncheon was held in the hall above Casey's bar. We were able to comfort Danny's family and mingle with the out of town Firefighters. It was a grand affair. It was a befitting party done in the Irish tradition of celebrating a joyous after life for Danny.

When the family left and the crowd thinned we went downstairs to Casey's bar. We ordered several pitchers of beer and started talking about the fire. We joked about how the cops had gotten trapped. Before long we were roaring with laughter over how things had gone from bad to worse than bad. We were not being disrespectful because we knew Danny's spirit was still with us. We were on our second round of beers when a young Firefighter from Engine 32 walked up to our table.

"Sorry about Danny," he said.

"I just want to let you guys know about something weird that happened the night Danny died. We had a run about three in the morning. It was foggy when we rolled out of quarters. I was on the driver's side of the rig putting on my fire coat. I glanced across the river at Belle Isle and thought I saw some large horses rearing up. Standing behind those horses was a Firefighter who lifted his helmet in the air and raised his arms in a victory sign. It was only for an instant but I am sure it happened."

There was silence at the table. I looked at Joe and we stared into each others eyes. He started to smile and so did I. When I looked at the other guys they were smiling too.

"Give this kid a beer," Joe shouted.

The End